american

ELF

*Jay! Live FRIEND.
LONG LIVER
Hope you ENJOY.*

american
ELF

TREY HAYNES

TATE PUBLISHING & *Enterprises*

American Elf
Copyright © 2009 by Trey Haynes. All rights reserved.

The opinions expressed by the author are not necessarily those of Tate Publishing, LLC.

Published by Tate Publishing & Enterprises, LLC
127 E. Trade Center Terrace | Mustang, Oklahoma 73064 USA
1.888.361.9473 | www.tatepublishing.com

Tate Publishing is committed to excellence in the publishing industry. The company reflects the philosophy established by the founders, based on Psalm 68:11,
"The Lord gave the word and great was the company of those who published it."

Book design copyright © 2009 by Tate Publishing, LLC. All rights reserved.
Cover design by Lindsay B. Behrens
Interior design by Joey Garrett

Published in the United States of America

ISBN: 978-1-60799-488-6
1. Fiction / General
2. Fiction / Humorous
09.06.09

acknowledgments

I acknowledge the friends and mentors who have helped inspire me on my scripts and stories, as well as providing ideas and assistance. I would like to thank Dewayne Henagar, Beverly Emmett, Emily Barclay, Chris Chaplin, Andrew Lim, Steve Thompson, Mimi Bilyeu, Tamela Ekstrom, Dixie Jordan, Trudy Rogers, Kynda Yates, Linda McDonald, Julie Bartness, my friends and partners at Tate Publishing, and, of course, Donna and Bob McKeegen for all their hard work with anything ever asked of them.

Thank you to my parents, Jim and Peggy Haynes, sister, Cori Osborn, brother, Mike Haynes, niece Sarah Stevens, as well as extended family, Russ Letchford, Richard McMillan, Hugh, Kathleen, and Cory Wheelus, and the Ryans and the Seegers. I'm surrounded by the most supportive family and one that I am truly proud of.

I would also like to acknowledge friends who have been like brothers to me: Scott Danemiller, Bryan Matula, Dan Dooling, Dave Hammon, Stace Harris, John Conley, and Jeff Stoabs, Joe Dorman, Steven Conway, Jeff Glass, Troy Redmon, Jimmy Cook, Steve Henne, Brent Byler, Tom Skinner, Joe Turner, and Jay Collins. The Beau's Wine Bin group, 66' Bowl group, BSF group, and my friends at the Integris Healthline and One Call.

Lastly, I'd like to acknowledge a friend who always made me laugh, did not take anything seriously, and will always be missed, Rick Bluhm.

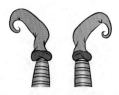

Strike Threatens Christmas

"Don't you want more money?" screams Birtnink.

Elves scurry to exit Santa's toy shop as a crooked union elf known for his shady deals, Birtnink, stands in the middle of the room on a workshop table, running his dirty, jagged fingernails through his greased back hair. He points at an elf who picks up his tools.

"Out!"

Birtnink hops off the table and paces the floor, taking credit for clearing out almost all of the elves in order to renegotiate a contract for *more money* from "Santa Inc." Uniforms are tossed in a pile in the corner of the room. A mouse rushes to go inside his hole in the wall but drops his glasses. He tries to retrieve them until *crunch*! Birtnink steps on and grinds them into the floor. Birtnink exits the room to work on his proposal. Two elves, out on break, re-enter the suddenly quiet and empty shop. Someone will need to replace the elves who are pretending to be ailing and putting Christmas at jeopardy.

The North Pole

Over snow-covered mountains, and the furthest Northern region on earth, a star illuminates a small yet bustling city below that is scaled down to half the size of a normal city. Even the inhabitants, mostly elves, are half-size, except for their ears, which are practically double normal size and come to a point. Smoke billows from factories toward the cold, gray sky and sleds slide and rush to get to their destination. A penguin, serious in nature and always on time, scoops up a newspaper, and flips through the pages as a curious elf leans over his shoulder. The annoyed penguin swats him away and continues to read, fumbling over the latest news and unaware of the big story that is soon to break and leaked to the North Pole media.

The main street is lined with a variety of shops as elves leave one and happily skip into another. A candy store bursts with colorful lollipops and gumdrops. Next door, a chocolate train races around a chocolate track inside the window display of a chocolate store.

Outside, a sled loaded with gifts races to beat the traffic light but almost hits another sled after the light turns red. A napping elf police officer, sitting in a police sled behind a billboard featuring a smiling Santa selling aluminum siding, decides to put on his lights and pursue the elf. Another sled makes its way safely past the buildings to a row of houses that dot the snowy, white landscape.

An elf checks his mail and makes his way inside his house as another chaotic day during the "busy season." Plumes of black and gray smoke pump out of chimney tops. Further off in the distance, past the row of houses, beyond the paved roads, over the waves of snow-banks, and nestled deep in the woods, a light flickers through a window of a large tree trunk. Snow falls gingerly in front of the door, laying a soft blanket on the doorstep and over a sleeping dog.

Grunting can be heard inside as Rowdy, a muscle-bound elf in a tank top, lifts a barbell above his head and accidentally knocks a lantern back and forth. "No compensation. No rewards. No recognition," he grumbles to himself. He drops the weights on the floor, narrowly missing another mouse and wearing thick glasses. The mouse adjusts his glasses, shakes his fist at Rowdy, and then scampers off.

"Sorry," Rowdy tells him. Rowdy is from a long line of worker elves. An accident to his father caused him to walk away from the job, thus breaking the chain. Rowdy has worked as an apprentice then worked his way up to head toy engineer to bring honor back to the family name.

Rowdy moves the weights aside and then looks in the mirror. The flattering mirror reflects a stockier and taller Rowdy. "Hmm. Not bad." Rowdy blows out a candle, puts a flannel shirt on, and leans down toward the mouse. "Take care of the place while I'm gone." Only a tiny squeaking noise can be heard back from the mouse, and Rowdy puts a small piece of cheese on a plate, complete with a tiny cup and utensils. "Don't worry, I'll be fine." He grabs a bag and his jacket and walks toward the door. He stops and looks back at his feeble father, who sits in a wheelchair staring out the window. "Bye, Dad."

His dad does not respond, and Rowdy walks out into the bitter cold. He steps over two mounds of snow and stops. "Hey..." he says, nudging the mounds. Two huskies stand up and stretch, only to go back to napping.

"Forget it, I'll walk." Rowdy walks down a winding path in the forest lined with trees that reach out far enough to brush up against him. His feet crunch with every step. Moans and screams echo from the mountains to the West and Rowdy looks up. An owl swivels its head and peers down on him with piercing eyes. Of all the dozens of times Rowdy had taken this path, this was the coldest and loneliest. He quickens his pace towards Santa's toyshop, a full night's walk away.

Not So Sunny Detroit

A group of teens push a rusty, old car down a street in Detroit. Buildings are boarded up and begin to decay. Choppy Christmas music cuts in and out of an old speaker perched on a warehouse of an area where the spirit of Christmas has clearly been left behind. A bundled up homeless man ducks down a back alley, disappearing into a smoky haze of building exhaust. Inside the warehouse, machines churn as metal parts move slowly down an assembly line. A rugged worker places a sheet of metal down and the machine chomps prematurely, almost taking off his hand. He rips his apron off and tosses it aside, yelling, "I've had enough of this!" He walks out and passes a large, hulking man with a permanent sweat line across his brow, Roy Hopkins is forty-four years old, but the worry lines make him appear older.

"I need you on the line," Roy says, more pleading than demanding.

"The equipment doesn't work. Parts don't fit. Just give up, Hoskins." He shakes his head and then walks out, much like many who have lost faith in Roy and the failing economy. Roy follows him a few steps until he passes a police officer who is escorting two lanky, jewelry-adorned, handcuffed Italian brothers, Frankie and Johnnie Barbozi. "Let me guess—overdue library books?" Roy tosses the apron onto a stack of others.

"You're a funny guy," Johnnie says as he struts closer to

Roy with loose bravado. Roy's been through this a million times before with the work release program a few
blocks away and he knows the routine. Roy's nose almost
touches Johnnie's. "Not as funny as you're gonna be if
you don't do as I say." Roy backs off, and Frankie and
Johnnie look at each other.

"They're in your custody for two weeks. Your favorite
work release program," the police officer tells Roy.

"Then you'll find someone else to deal with them?"

"Yeah, sure." The police officer takes the cuffs off,
and Johnnie rubs out the numbness in his wrist. "What's
he talking about?" Johnnie whispers as he leans closer to
Frankie. Frankie smacks Johnnie across the head. "No
more trouble, Johnnie." Frankie winks at Roy, but Roy is
already walking back to his office. "Halfway house, huh?"
Roy asks.

"Going straight." Johnnie tells him.

"So you two are a little funny?" Roy looks back.
Johnnie and Frankie look at each other and then back at
Roy. "No, no." Johnnie punches Frankie in the arm.

"Tough guys!" Frankie punches Johnnie across the
chin, almost knocking him out.

Roy rolls his eyes and walks toward his office but stops
at a thermostat on the wall. He turns it back down to
sixty-five degrees. "Who keeps messin' with my thermostat?" He walks off and Wayne, fellow employee, mus-
cular and always wearing his shirts a size too small, turns it
back up.

Santa's Serene Toy Shop

An elf wearing cowboy boots and a five gallon hat wipes the chewing tobacco off of his chin and then throws hay into a trough for reindeer as they trot over. One young male reindeer is caught behind the pack and decides to leap over the rest to the front of the line but falls short, falling in the middle of the herd and receiving some glares from the older reindeer as he is nudged forcibly to the back. The leathery elf cowboy climbs on top of the fence, and points the reindeer to the back of the line. Its nose faintly lights up as it trots back. He picks up a harness on the ground and hands it over the fence to another elf, who takes it to a huge building with Santa's living quarters, elf bunk rooms, warehouse, cafeteria, and workshop with multiple fireplaces for the most extreme cold temperatures. A small puff of smoke floats out of the top of Santa's workshop until a toy plane hits it and it disintegrates. He walks past a snowman and tips his hat, and then walks in a side door and disappears down a long hall, taking the harness to be repaired.

The workshop is a place where gifted elves work fantastically fast to build toys that they were trained to do since birth, but it is unusually quiet five days before Christmas. A mouse stitches a soft leather football. Unfinished toy soldiers lie in a heap on a wood table. An elf coughs, then puts a wheel on a red wagon and spins it. The light hits it, and red fires out in all directions.

An elf paints an eye on a toy soldier and hands it back but no one is there. He slides over to the empty table to complete the soldier alone.

Roy's Warehouse

Flames scream out of the side of a machine in the Detroit warehouse as Crane, a skinny man in his late fifties, who shuffles when he walks and sweats profusely, rushes over to extinguish the flames.

"Uh, Roy?" He struggles with the situation, but then, this is a typical reaction for Crane, who only works there to help out his buddy Roy for minimal pay. "We have some problems over here."

Crane runs back and grabs a fire extinguisher and squeezes the trigger … nothing.

He tosses it aside and runs back and grabs another fire extinguisher but it also is empty. Crane runs around frantically while another employee throws a blanket over the small fire and turns the machine off. Crane almost collapses, sweat dripping from his nose. "Thanks."

Gonna Need Backup ... Elves

A pair of socks runs away from Santa's hands that can't quite reach them until they are finally snatched up.

Black boots are slipped on over the socks and Santa walks out his bedroom door and into the toy shop. Long wooden tables have toy parts strewn about them. One elf carries a large box through the workshop, as a mouse tightens a screw in a robot. Spit hits Santa's boots and a towel cracks against them as an elf shoe-shine boy kneels. "I can shine those for ya."

The shoeshine boy is brushed away by Santa's large hand. Santa takes a step and the wood floor creaks and crackles under the weight.

A banana drops to the floor. Santa reaches for it but quickly gives up after falling short because of his robust size.

Santa looks over the floor as only four elves rush frantically around the room trying to assemble toys. Santa steps out. "Where are my workers?"

Bristo, a two foot tall elder elf with a gray mustache, beard, and bulging eyes who looks more like a garden gnome, stands in the middle of the empty floor. He tries to speak but is terrified as Santa towers over him.

An elf slips on the banana and slides into a stack of toys, sending them flying in all directions. Santa rubs his temples and returns his attention to Bristo, who is still having trouble with the words. His mouth almost seems to swell, and Santa slowly leans down to go eye level with him. "Slow," Santa tells him.

"They're all sick," Bristo finally blurts out in a high-pitched voice.

The elf shoeshine boy picks at his teeth with a toothpick. "You got a problem."

Birtnink runs to the middle of the room and points at the shoeshine boy, who is quickly loading up his belongings. "How did he get in here?" Birtnink screams.

The elf shoeshine boy runs out through a hole in the wall to one of the many underground tunnels built hundreds of years ago below the factory. "I want that boarded up!" Santa looks around the empty room and checks underneath the assembly line. "I want to know where my men are!"

Corky, a taller elf at almost four feet tall with enormous ears, looks up from the assembly line and holds a teddy bear leg. "I'm feeling a little woozy myself." Corky lets out a faint cough.

"Get back to work, Cork!" Santa stomps off down the hall toward a door with a "Do Not Disturb" sign on it. The door swings open, and Santa's eyes become wide as he looks over the elf bunkroom. Forty to fifty elves lay in a bed that stretches into the distance, the end is barely visible. All of the elves have thermometers in their mouths and slowly slip under the covers, shivering as they try to cover their heads with a thick, fluffy, white blanket.

Santa, mixed with emotions and anxiety, sits on the edge of the bed, tilting it underneath his weight. Elves start to roll his way until he decides to stand back up and the bed falls flat. "We only have four days before Christmas."

The elves slowly peek from beneath the covers. Santa grabs a sick elf's thermometer.

"Didn't you take the precautions?" He shakes the thermometer and checks it.

"Maybe it was something in the cider?" Birtnink gives a sly wink to a couple of the elves.

"I drank that cider." Santa barks back at them when Rowdy storms into the room.

"What the heck is going on here?" Rowdy dashes in front of the bed and inspects the elves. Birtnink tries to cut him off but is a little intimidated by the stocky elf.

"How dare a working-class commoner question the acts of the chosen few?" Birtnink goes to the mirror. The mirror elongates his nose and he gives it a scowl. "Shouldn't you be out with the hired help? You know … outside the fence." Birtnink asks Rowdy. Santa runs his hands through his beard as Rowdy turns, his little butt crack exposed. A robot makes its way across the room. "Let's play … let's play … let's—" Rowdy turns and kicks the toy robot across the floor catapulting it over Birtnink's head. It shatters against the wall, and the pieces rain down on elves. "Rowdy!" Santa screams at him but he is already out the door. Santa looks back down at the bed and elves quickly shimmy under the covers. He can only shake his head. "Why me?"

Santa notices an elf wearing a lab jacket and standing to the side. He was hired by Birtnink and part of Birtnink's plan. "Who are you?" Santa asks.

The elf looks toward Birtnink. "I'm a doctor."

"I don't know you … what are your credentials?"

The elf, panicked, looks over at Birtnink again.

"You're not our physician! Get out of here."

The elf rushes out when Birtnink goes to Santa with

a deeply sympathetic and concerned look. "Our physician had a family emergency and he was filling in."

Santa stomps out as Birtnink turns back to the elves and gives a big thumbs-up.

The room is quiet and tense, though the smell of freshly baked bread and cookies flows from the next room where Mrs. Claus cooks away. Santa stares out the window of his dining room as the elders sit around the large oak table that is filled with milk and cookies on one plate and fruit on the other. Santa begins to speak and his stomach rumbles and roars loudly as the elves try not to notice. Santa waits a moment and starts in again, but it makes even more noise. Santa grabs a cookie and bites into it as an apple slice is placed in front of him. He tosses it behind him.

Otto, an overweight elf in a disheveled business suit and bow tie that hangs loosely off his neck, flips through notes with no regard to the contents. Rowdy paces behind the table, his boots clacking with every small step. Birtnink leans across the table and knowingly suggests the impossible and ridiculous. "Maybe we could negotiate at a later date."

Birtnink begins to lay out a contract with his provisions on it when Santa slaps the table in front of him. "What kind of answer is that?" Crumbs fly from the corners of his mouth. Otto throws the papers in the air. "Tell the elves to go back to work!" The elder elves pretend to read their memos and avoid eye contact.

Santa, stern but almost defeated, looks over the elder elves. "I can't force them to work."

Corky mumbles under his breath. "It never stopped you before … you sweatshop working, under appreciating, tub of—" Corky is hit in the head with a cookie. Rowdy wipes his hands off. Santa runs his hands through his wavy white hair and to his surprise, pulls out a small toy soldier. He tosses it aside and leans on the table. "They've never been this sick."

Corky raises his hand. "Actually, Santa, last year—"

"I'm not talking about the past! Now come up with a solution!" Santa sits in his large leather chair and eases back. Mrs. Claus runs in the room with a tray full of sliced fruit and Santa rolls his eyes. "Please, Mrs. Claus," he tells her as she lays the tray down and walks out.

Corky raises his hand again. "How about we recruit some workers?"

Bristo, eyes bulging more than usual and trembling, looks toward Santa. Santa slowly stands while glaring at Corky. "What did you say?" Two elder elves look at each other as another elf crawls under the table. Rowdy bursts out. "Let's recruit from within the city. I have some men, who haven't passed the test and don't have the family history, but—"

Birtnink slams his fists on the table and scowls at Rowdy, who is normally looked on as an outsider but also a much-needed toy engineer in the final days before Christmas.

"It's against all our bylaws." Birtnink flips through his documents and pulls out the page and holds it up.

Rowdy turns to Santa. "I'm tired of our bylaws." This draws a gasp from the group, but Rowdy doesn't turn away from Santa until Birtnink scrambles around the table to Santa. "Why can't we give the elves what they need?" Birtnink shies away with his patented sympathetic expression; his lower lip trembles. "Maybe a little more of an incentive." He turns and slyly grins to himself. Rowdy looks up at Santa and then down at Birtnink. "Is that why they're sick, Birt?" Birtnink turns slowly to Rowdy, his nose throwing a shadow across the room. He looks Rowdy up and down. "The name is Birtnink. Shouldn't you be shoveling reindeer poop like your father did until he had that untimely accident?"

Rowdy pops his knuckles but takes a deep breath, hops out of his chair, shoots Birtnink a glare, and heads for the door until Santa states, "I'm putting Rowdy in charge."

"What?" Birtnink exclaims as his ears slowly droop.

"What?" Rowdy asks Santa, who swivels around in his chair and faces the wall.

"Who is in charge of the labor commission?" Otto shuffles through papers and mumbles to himself as he raises his hand. "I am." Santa lets out a moan and Otto continues, as he's talking more to himself than addressing the others. "Mexico has a few … No, they're ready." Not Germany. No, though Stuttgart is lovely this time of year." Otto holds up a list with a sight of relief. "Here it is!" The elders look up. "Laundry list I lost." More moans as he studies it for a brief moment and tosses it aside. He digs again. "Aha." He pulls out a document. "Finland, Sir." He looks up. "Yes, Finland is on call and should have workers trained and ready to go at a moments notice." Otto wipes the sweat off his forehead, then reaches for his flask, fumbling and dropping it causing a loud thud and rattling against the wooden floor.

"I'll send for them." Santa stands and rubs his belly and then scratches. He continues. "Rowdy can bring a few workers. A few," he emphasizes. "They can stay on the premises for four days."

Birtnink stands on his chair. "They're not qualified!"

Santa, his nerves frazzled, grips the end of the table

and it shakes under the elves' chins. "I need workers and I need them fast."

Santa reaches under the fruit and grabs a cookie. He mumbles to himself while staring out the window. "Experts in the field ... " Santa's voice trails off.

Foreclosure

Jimbo, a large black man with a gentle and playful disposition, walks by Crane and slowly reaches down toward his shoulder. "Don't you even," Crane tells him, but too late. He grabs Crane by the shoulder and then wets his finger and sticks it in his ear. Crane, looking as though his scrawny frame will break in half, screams to break free of his grasp. "Four days till Christmas," Jimbo tells him and then adds, "You seen Hoskins?"

Crane looks around the warehouse. "He was here earlier. You lookin' for him?"

"Trying to avoid him."

Crane continues to look. "Do you plan on working today?"

"*It's a Wonderful Life* is on tonight. You're more than welcome to come over." Jimbo puts his tools away and grabs his timecard. "Gonna stay and help Roy," Crane tells him.

"Suit yourself." Jimbo picks up his thermos. "And don't call me tonight, even if the place is on fire."

Time to Fly

Santa stands at the foot of the door with Otto, who is wearing his favorite pinstripe business suit. Santa follows him out. "Stay out of the bars." Otto walks away with his briefcase in tow.

"I mean it, Otto." Santa tells him.

Otto smiles, but mutters under his breath. "You stay away from cookies and red meat."

"I heard that!" Santa returns his attention to an elf mechanic, whose leg hangs out from under a machine. "Hey! What are you doing down there?" Santa grabs his legs and drags him out, "No changes without my permission."

Otto skips a couple of steps as he reaches the North Pole airport located a couple of blocks away. Santa follows a little behind as he assists Bristo who will travel with him. Otto looks in all directions until he spots Birtnink in one of the hangars entering a sled.

Birtnink hands the elf pilot an envelope as promised and shakes his hand. He swings the door open to exit the sled and almost knocks Otto over. Birtnink quickly rushes off under Santa's watchful eye as he finally arrives with Bristo.

The elf pilot wearing goggles and head gear steers, checks the instruments. Otto climbs in and saunters down the aisle in the government sled used specifically for the labor commission, where seats are laced in satin and were purchased at triple the price of a normal sled. Santa assists Bristo up the stairs and safely into one of the front seats. Santa looks back at Otto.

"I'm warning you Otto. Just pick up our workers and get back quickly." Santa sets a watch with a small cuckoo clock on it that pecks on his wrist every hour on the hour. Santa backs away as the sled is pulled out of the hangar and taxied down a runway with reindeer clacking their hoofs in the lead. Another sled lands and moves swiftly by them as an elf gets the okay from the tower and leads them on another runway. The elf pilot turns the steering column and speaks into his headset.

"Prepare for takeoff."

The sled jerks back and forth and begins its climb. The sled slices through clouds as it continues upward. They pass through another cloud and Otto stares out the side and hums to himself. The stars sparkle in the distance.

"Lovely evening." He grabs a magazine, *Elf Weekly,* but quickly tosses it aside.

"Can we—"

The elf pilot comes over the speaker. "You are free to move about the cabin."

Otto goes to the back and pours himself a drink. He glances toward Bristo. "Like one?" Bristo looks his way and Otto waves him off.

"Forget it." He sits down again. "Looks like we're gonna be up here for awhile. Otto grabs the telescope and looks out over the mountains. A small Indian village glistens below. The sled slices through clouds and dodges a falling star. Outside, the lead deer kicks and leans toward the left. His nose lights up the sky. Otto finishes his drink and takes out his flask. He turns it upside down and notices it is empty. He moans and makes his

way to the cart in the back. Much to his disappoint-
ment, it is littered with empty bottles (probably from his
last trip) and a fidgety Otto lets out a sigh. He finds a
little left in a bottle and pours himself a drink. He raises
the glass to his perched lips until the sled jerks and he
spills the drink on himself. Otto goes back and pulls out
his telescope, peering out the side again until his eyelids
become heavy and slowly shut. The elf pilot comes over
the speaker again. "We're having a little trouble with the
landing gear and will make a quick stop in Detroit. The
sled goes swiftly down over a residential neighborhood.
Otto stretches and looks outside. He sees a marquee
outside a bowling alley with, "dollar longnecks" lit up in
blinking red lights. He looks up as if not sure if he trusts
his eyesight and looks again. The sled dives downward
through a cloud. Bristo rolls down the aisle.

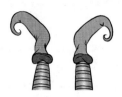

An Unlikely Place
to Recruit Elves

At the hubcap factory, Roy wipes the sweat from his forehead and the tired from his eyes. His fingernails are caked in black gunk. "Can't figure out what is wrong." He drops the wrench to his side when Crane moves in next to him and studies the equipment. "It's this old equipment, Roy."

Roy fidgets with it until he cuts his hand, quickly pulling it away. He wraps it with a rag and goes back for more. "I know I can fix it."

Crane backs off. "The men are tired." Crane waits for Roy's response as Roy squats to get a better view at the broken equipment and then throws the rag down. Roy stands and avoids Crane's advice. "I hate to be the one to tell ya, Roy, but it ain't gonna work."

Roy starts walking away but Sutter—menacing, hulking, and covered in tattoos—cuts him off. Roy turns one way and then the next, but Sutter moves with him in almost a clumsy dance. "I'm not coming back this time, Roy. And I want my money."

"Sutter, please … I'm having a hard time."

Wayne goes to Roy's defense like he usually does, and probably more because of his disdain for Sutter. "You'll get it when we do, Scrooge." Wayne flexes and Sutter walks away. Wayne turns back to the Roy. "When do we get paid, Roy?"

Wayne follows Roy as he walks back to his office and checks the thermostat. Wayne turns it back up and walks to the break room bathroom with the newspaper. Roy sits in his office that has old parts strewn around and stacks of papers and unpaid bills on the desk. He flips over a newspaper with the headlines, "More Layoffs Expected." Not having the desire to take in any more bad news about the economy, he picks up a hubcap and stares at his distorted reflection. He puts a spring in the middle and spins it. He speaks into it and his voice echoes. Wallace Von Hubert … the fourth … maybe the fifth, thirties, and from a bloodline of corrupt money that goes back centuries laced with crooked deals, taps on the door. "I didn't come at a bad time, did I?"

Roy tosses the hubcaps aside and grumbles to himself while he tries to find something to look busy and avoiding eye contact.

"Important meeting … with yourself?" Wallace chuckles to himself.

"You can build your sports stadium, or condos, or whatever you're planning somewhere else." Roy tells him, but Wallace, brushing objects away as if they carry a disease, moves closer to the desk. "Not this cheap, Roy." He looks closer at an old picture of Roy's bowling team and lays it facedown. "This is an industrial wasteland."

"So you plan on taking a low-rent area, buy it up for cheap, and move the poor?" Roy asks.

"Like rats," Wallace answers and then winks at Roy. "They'll find another place to live. They always do." Wallace dusts off the chair and starts to sit down, but sets his briefcase down instead. "Roy, you employ ex-

cons—not even good ones at that—high school drop-
outs, and transients."

Wallace sits on the corner of Roy's desk. "Take the
money, sweetheart. Go home to your family."

"Ten million," Roy tells him, and Wallace, surprised,
almost knocks a picture off the wall but catches it and
places it back. He wipes his hands on a scarf. "I wish I
could." Roy knows his deceitful nature and will try every
option to keep Wallace away. Wallace runs his hand
along the lining of his suit. "Like the suit? I can get you
one. Even for your size."

"Ten million is nothing, considering what you'll pay
for the stadium." Roy shuts his briefcase and stands up.

"What's the next project, Roy? Uh, automotive parts,
ball bearings, little red wagons?"

"We're done." Roy grabs Wallace's briefcase and
tosses it outside. Wallace's conniving friendly demeanor
is replaced with anger and venom. "Have you been talking to anyone else?" Wallace asks him as he walks to the
door.

"I'm gonna make this place work."

Wallace picks up his briefcase.

"One week, Roy. Then I'll deal with the bank."

He's given Roy hollow threats before, but Roy knows
this one is for real.

Stranger in Town

Otto lugs his briefcase with one hand and holds a drink with the other as he passes the theater with Bristo struggling to keep up behind him. "Let's get out of here," Otto tells him. A drunk and dirty Santa stumbles out of the theater with a beer in one hand and a cigar in the other. Otto looks in his direction. "Santa?"

The dirty Santa walks inside the bowling alley. Otto points. "To the bowling alley!" Otto runs to the opposite side of the street, with Bristo trying to avoid the large puddles and snow drifts that come up to his chin. At the factory, Wayne turns off the last light, and Crane lays a broom against the wall. Crane walks to the office and winks at Roy. "Where does a guy go when he's down on his luck, needs companionship, and wants to vent some anger?" Sound of bowling pins crashing. It's bowling night for the guys, one of the few places of solace from the outside world.

Bowling shoes that reek of disinfectant are given out at the front desk. The bartender watches the television as Otto sips on a beer and Bristo sits on the barstool beside him, clutching his suitcase with both hands and legs dangling from the bar stool. Otto, gripping the side of the bar and glossy-eyed, looks in Bristo's direction. "Last one. Promise." Otto goes back to the beer and struggles to lift the mug. Bristo blurts out, "Drunk."

"Shut up, Bristo. Enjoy life once in awhile." Otto

looks to the bartender. "Cold frosty, please!" *Burrrrrrp.*
The bartender grabs another mug and looks them over.

"You boys don't look like you're from around
here ... Cleveland?"

Otto looks at him and then at Bristo. "Uh, yeah."

Santa nibbles on a huge pile of cookies when Mrs. Claus
pulls it away and slips him some apple slices. He stares
straight ahead. "Christmas is ruined."

She runs her hands through his hair, which usually
helps him relax or even at times, fall fast asleep.

"You sent Otto to retrieve some men, didn't you?" she
asks.

Santa begins to cry. "Christmas is ruined." Mrs. Claus
goes to hug Santa, who hangs his head that feels like a
weight.

"Ruined."

Replacements?

Crane and Roy walk through the glass doors with their bowling bags. Crane slaps Roy on the shoulder and tries to get him to cheer up. "Let's not worry about the factory and enjoy a game of bowling."

Otto looks up from his beer, froth covering his face like a beard and moustache. "Factory?" Otto hands the bartender his empty glass and then hops off the barstool. It takes Bristo a little longer as he lays flat on it and then gently lowers himself to the ground. Roy's bitter wife, Judy, stands at the entrance with their five-year-old son, Sam. Otto walks toward Roy, but is unintentionally cut off by Judy. Otto taps on Roy's leg. "Excuse me." Judy has already got Roy's attention, and Crane pretends to find a ball on the rack, regardless of the fact he brought his own. "I'm taking Sam to my parents." Judy takes Sam by the hand and begins to walk off, but Roy grabs them. "Wait a minute, Judy."

Otto squeezes in between them as Sam goes wide-eyed standing next to him. Sam looks down at his elf shoes. "Probably need a good polish," Otto tells Sam.

"He needs a real father, Roy. Not one who hangs out at that failing factory day and night," Judy tells Roy, who tries to shove Otto out of the way. Otto bites his hand.

"Owww! I'm gonna make it work."

Judy breaks away. "You know how many times I've heard that, Roy?"

Roy looks down at Sam and then back at the guys, who are all watching but quickly divert their attention.

"People depend on me." Roy pleads to her.

Judy gives him an insincere half-face smile. "I'm going away, Roy." She takes Sam's hand, and Otto goes back to tapping Roy on the leg.

"I'll only take a moment of your time," Otto tells him, but Roy shoves him away again. "Not in the mood."

Judy stops and looks back. "You never are." She opens the door, and Sam waves goodbye. "Not you, Judy," he calls out to Sam. "How did your football game go?"

"Typical, Roy." Judy shakes her head and walks off.

"He doesn't play football," Judy tells him.

"Basketball? Fencing? Auto racing?" Roy asks. "What?" he asks, throwing up his arms. No change.

"I'm only five," Sam tells Roy before he is whisked away.

Stress ... for Santa

Santa paces in his room moving from side to side like a pendulum. He runs his hands through his beard, and a chunk of hair goes with it. Tossing it aside, he thumps himself in the forehead. "Think, darn you." He grabs a handful of cookies, cupcakes, and jelly beans, shoves them in his mouth, and resumes pacing.

Outside the room in the adjoining toy shop, the walls shake and rumble until a clock falls off the wall and onto an elf sleeping on the job. The clock quickly drags itself away. Mrs. Claus frantically puts a blood pressure cuff on Santa's arm and starts pumping. "I might just fire all the elves," Santa tells Mrs. Claus, who takes the cuff of his arm and Santa paces again. "They might hear you," she tells him.

"I don't care! Fire all of ya! *All of ya!*" Santa screams toward the door. Mrs. Claus takes out a thermometer. "I'm switching you to decaf." She sticks the thermometer in his mouth, and it rapidly bubbles at the top.

Unshaven and unkempt elves yell and cheer in the elf bunk room as they are crouched beside the bed. Money is tossed beside two gingerbread men who wrestle. One of the gingerbread men bites into the other. It becomes quiet until he lets go. Icing runs off of the other gingerbread man's shoulder, and the yelling and tossing of money in the center continues until Birtnink walks in unnoticed. "He's desperate, but not desperate enough."

Birtnink announces. They don't pay attention to him until he steps in front of the gingerbread men. "I said—*oww!*" He looks down at the gingerbread men biting on his ankle. An elf springs up. "Tell us later, *Birtstink*." The elves laugh and throw their money in a pile as Birtnink goes back to the door. Birtnink mumbles under his breath. "You ungrateful little…owww!" Birtnink grabs his ears and the gingerbread men cling to them with their mouths. The elves laugh and roll on the bed as Birtnink tosses them off and storms out.

Bowling and Beers

Bristo stands in the corner of the bowling alley clutching his briefcase as Otto staggers toward the bowling lanes with a beer in his hands. Roy walks to the bowling lane and kisses his bowling ball. "You're mine tonight."

Crane takes his old bowling shoes out and slides them on. "Shouldn't include your bowling ball in your fantasies."

"Shut up, Crane, and get focused on your game." Roy takes his first step but is grabbed by Otto. "You again?" Roy goes back to the lane. "I don't find Wallace's little joke funny."

Wayne messes up Otto's hair. "No pun intended." Wayne laughs to himself and, as usual, is the only one. Roy runs into Baby Ralph, his overweight bowling partner who lives with his mom. His stomach hangs out underneath his dirty T-shirt. "Want me to take care of 'em, Roy?"

Roy tries to squeeze around Baby Ralph, but has trouble. "No, but thank you."

Baby Ralph studies Otto as a small amount of spit clings to the corner of Baby Ralph's bottom lip. "Funny lookin' little critter."

Otto stomps on Baby Ralph's foot. "I demand a little respect here!" Roy tries to maneuver around Baby Ralph, the bowlers seating area, and Otto. Roy looks at Baby

Ralph, who can't seem to take his eyes off Otto. "Will you please move?"

Baby Ralph's beer rains down on Crane's bowling shoes, causing Crane to jerk them away and accidentally shoves Otto into Roy. "What? What do you want from me?" Roy screams as bowlers and bar slugs stop what they are doing. The bartender leans over the counter and asks Otto, "You gonna pay for those beers?" Roy signals him to put Otto's beers on his tab and finally makes his way around and sits at a table behind the lanes. Crane sits down and is followed by Wayne.

Bristo, wide-eyed and still clutching his briefcase, remains in the corner of the bar. Otto finally has Roy's attention. "I need eight strong workers for our factory." Roy pushes his seat out, screeching against the wood. "You want my workers?"

"Just for three or four days, though. The bartender said you were the one in charge." Sutter leans over from the opposite end of the bar. "Depends on who you talk to."

Roz, a burly woman in her forties wearing a large, worn-out jacket, drops her ball on the rack. Roz is the homeless person Wallace was referring to, but only by choice as she takes on temporary residence under a bridge in a box. She helps Roy around the shop but rarely accepts payment and acquires her property from discarded items found in salvage yards and garbage cans. After a family tragedy, she lost everything, including a successful business, only to resurface in Detroit and find companionship with Roy and the guys. Her rugged demeanor makes it difficult for anyone to get too close. Roz takes her bowling shoes out of the pocket in the jacket that hangs to the floor. "We gonna bowl or what?"

She lights a half-burned cigarette and then points at Otto. "Who's the little girl?"

A drunk woman stumbles up to Bristo, who avoids her glare. She leans down and almost loses her balance. "Don't think you're gonna get away with it this time. I'd slap you if I wasn't the lady that I am." She begins to hug Bristo but pulls herself away. "I'm sorry it didn't work out, Sugar." She staggers off and Otto goes to Bristo.

"Get a beer. Loosen up, will ya? You're already a hit with the ladies." He turns back to Roy.

"We can't really pay money," he said, talking to himself. "I guess we could. We could grant you a gift."

Bristo crawls up on the bar stool and is finally ready for his drink that he signals for.

"You want me to shut down my factory, take my employees, and go to some unknown land for four days ... and all for a gift?" Roy says, towering over Otto.

"Well, yeah."

Sutter slaps down on the pool table. "I'll do it." The bartender slides a mug down the bar that hits Bristo, and the both of them go flying over the edge of the bar, splashing beer straight up.

"Now wait a minute!" Roy barks out.

"One more, please." Otto looks back at the guys and chuckles. "How many times
have I used that one?"

North Pole? Roy tells himself as he ponders the thought.

The bartender looks at Roy, who is fishing through Otto's briefcase. "I'm about to close my doors, too, Roy. Maybe this gift will be worth something." The bartender shines a glass and pours Otto another drink. Sutter taps the pool stick on the floor, and Roy grabs the stick and tosses it across the table.

"You guys think he's actually from the North Pole?" Roy goes to Otto's luggage and rummages through it.

"Don't see why not," Crane tells him. Roy pulls out a teddy bear, toy soldier, elf hat, elf pants, gift-wrapping paper, ribbons, bottle of whiskey, and a long scroll. Otto grabs the bottle of whiskey.

"Forgot I had that."

The men and Roz gather around as Roy unwinds the scroll and the bartender hands Otto his drink. "Don't bother reading it," Otto tells them as he points at the scroll that is written in unusual marks and symbols. "You guys know how to run an assembly line, don't know you?"

Baby Ralph taps Otto on the shoulder, almost knocking him over. "Roy makes hubcap spokes." Otto takes a long drink off of his beer, gives the room a long, hard look, and thinks about it for a moment. "Good enough." Otto takes a piece of crystal and tosses it to Crane. Otto flattens out the scroll and signals for Crane to read it to the group. Crane places the crystal flat against the scroll. The lettering at the top reads, "To whom it may concern."

Wayne walks up to the bar, scratching himself. "How *did* you get here, little buddy?"

Otto stands on the bar. "Sled." He is pulled off the counter by large hands and escorted out.

Otto tries to go back inside. Roy grabs him by the collar and Crane carries his bag. "Just one more ... I mean it this time." Otto starts to take a drag off a cigarette, but Roy takes it out of his mouth and throws it in the snow. "Where is it?"

"Where's what?" Otto asks and Roy grabs him, almost lifting him off the ground.

"Sled! Where's your sled?"

The guys follow Otto around as he looks in a back alley. "What is that?" Crane asks.

A reindeer stands besides a building. Its nose illuminates the alley, and when the reindeer turns towards them, it almost blinds them. It leans down and buries its nose in the snow. They inch closer and see the shadow of six reindeer. Large horns throw shadows the length of the alley. Roy moves closer, not sure of what he is experiencing. "Could it be?"

Otto runs in front of a twenty-foot sled. "What, you think I was lying?"

Roy slides his hand along the sled that is lined in gold and red felt on the sides. He pushes it and it rocks back and forth. Otto rushes to the side of the sled and lays out the scroll and takes out his eyepiece. "You'd think I'd know this by now."

The guys move closer. Otto reads it to himself but looks up at the guys. "Not unless you sign off on all accidents, loss of time frame."

Crane taps him on the shoulder. "Loss of time frame?"

"That's if we accidentally send you back to medieval times. Extremely rare." Otto doesn't seem to be particularly concerned about their anxiety.

"What was that about accidents?" Wayne asks.

"Heavy equipment. Freezing temperatures. Let me get back to the list. Ear, nose, and throat transformation."

"Ear transformation?" Wayne asks again.

Otto points at his pointy ears and then his voice becomes much higher. "Voice changes, (then lower) that sort of thing. Get it?" Otto clears his throat and then spits.

Otto thinks about it, then looks back at the list. "Of course, confidentiality."

"What the heck…count me in," Roz tells them.

"Now wait a minute," Roy tells them.

"What do we have to lose?" Crane asks Roy.

Otto pulls out a candy cane that seeps with red out of the end. "Look, guys. I'm already late. If you don't want to do it, then I'm sure Santa will understand."

"Santa Claus?" Sutter blurts out.

"Have you been listening?" Otto rolls up the scroll.

Frankie looks at Roy and then at Otto, who is getting impatient. "We get paid?"

"I've already discussed that," Otto tells them.

"A gift or wish, something like that," says Roy.

Otto laughs to himself. "I'm not a genie." Otto puts the scroll in his briefcase. "Your wife and kids won't be back until Christmas Eve," Roy tells Crane. Crane's head dips down. "Something we gotta talk about, Roy." Crane goes on, avoiding troubling Roy with his problems at home. "Was gonna go hunting."

Otto jumps in the middle of them and pulls out a pen. "Only factory workers. We don't have time to train," Otto explains. "And no union representatives!"

Baby Ralph starts to cry. "What the heck is wrong?" asks Roy.

"My mom would…" Baby Ralph tells him and Otto rolls his eyes

"We understand, Baby."

"Probably best someone stays behind in case they don't make it back home."

Roy turns his attention to Otto. "Give us ten minutes." Roy runs back down the alley and goes to the left. He can be seen running back to the right. "The clock is ticking!" Otto tells him.

A man stands at his doorway laughing at Roy. "North Pole, huh?"

Sutter mocks Roy from the man's front yard. "Elves! Ha! Crazy talk."

Roy gives the man a playful jab. "Yeah, it's a joke. Have a happy holiday."

"Let me know when the Easter bunny comes around." The man shuts the door and Roy passes Sutter, who is enjoying this as Roy goes to the bowling alley.

The bright blue screen reflects off of Jimbo's face. Jimbo leans forward and slaps his knee when there is a knock on the door. He turns back and yells out, "Not here!" The volume is turned up. Crane peers in the window. "We need ya for something."

Jimbo screams back, "Not going hunting!"

It's a Wonderful Life with Jimmy Stewart kneeling next to his daughter is on television. Jimbo mutters, almost pouting, "Not gonna go." Jimbo runs to the window and shuts the blinds. He eases back in the chair and laughs at the show when he catches something in the corner of his eye. Crane stands in the doorway. "You left the back door unlocked."

Wayne shows up with bags and Otto stands next to the sled holding a list. Jimbo, blindfolded, steps up to the sled with Crane. Crane takes off his blindfold. "What is—*whoa!*" Jimbo almost collapses when Otto hands him a clipboard and pen. "Sign here."

Jimbo scribbles his name but doesn't take his eyes off the sled. Roy leads Frankie and Johnnie.

"Like to know what's going on." Johnnie stops as he sees the red glare off of the lead reindeer's nose. "It's a trick!" Panicked from the red light, Frankie and Johnnie turn and collide, both falling to the ground and writhing in pain. Otto bites his lip and has second thoughts. "Oh, boy. Maybe I can still get to Finland." Johnnie and Frankie slowly stand, and Frankie steps in front of Roy.

"Roy, this is a prisoner release program. Doesn't mean that you can …"

"Get in the sled." Roy tells him and Frankie makes his way inside.

"Okay." Roy takes a step inside. "Let's do this."

Otto checks his lists. "No! No! No!" He slaps the list at his side and yanks on Roy's sleeve. "We still need one more."

"We can do the job of eight," Roy tells him.

Otto shakes his head. "Dear, dear. I hate to unload …" Sutter tosses his bag aboard and grabs the list out of Otto's hands. He marks an "X" on it and then jams the list in Otto's pocket. Roy follows behind him, and Otto pulls the door shut. The sled jerks a little, and the reindeer move down the back alley, dragging the sled behind them.

The elf pilot comes over the loudspeaker. "Welcome to Elf Air."

The guys and Roz sit back on the red felt seats when Sutter shuts the rack, holding his luggage. They move aside for him.

Otto stands in the aisle and waves his hands like a flight attendant. "Exits are on the side. There will be no food or drink. Lean all seats up for takeoff, blah, blah, blah. You guys know the drill." The reindeer start pulling the sled faster.

"*Destination North Pole!*"

Dirty Santa urinates in the back alley, but watches the sled pass by in a flash. Baby Ralph smacks Dirty Santa to join him in saluting the sled.

Time to Prepare for the Experts

Santa stands over some female elves who stitch small jackets. A female looks toward Santa and asks in a high-pitched, squeaky voice, "Big enough?"

Santa holds up the tiny outfit. "Lots bigger." Santa walks toward the window and looks up at a large clock on the wall that stretches its arms until it catches Santa's glare. It quickly corrects itself. "According to my calculations, my toy experts should be on their way now."

The guys brace themselves as the cabin shifts back and forth and Frankie, turning a light shade of green, clutches the side with his eyes closed. "I think I'm gonna be sick!"

Something clicks in Wayne's head, judging by his expression, and he snaps his fingers as he watches Frankie. "I knew there was something I remembered about you ... St. Francis ... class of '88?"

"Shut up, Wayne," Johnnie tells him as Roy points at the brothers. "I want you two in my sights at all times."

The elf pilot comes over the loudspeaker. "We'll, uh ... be experiencing ... uh ... slight turbulence."

Frankie, pale and drenched in sweat, waves at Roy. "May I have permission to get sick?"

"No!" Roy barks at him as the top rolls open, revealing small patches of clouds and stars. Warm air engulfs them. Roz stands and Crane reaches out to grab her. "Watch that left hand, buddy."

Otto looks back and smiles. "She'll be fine."

Roz winks at Crane. "But, if it makes you feel better."

A large ball of flames that was once a star moves quickly by them, then disintegrates into thousands of sparkles. Crane looks over the side. "I can't believe it." Crane looks back and forth as if not to be noticed, then spits over the side. Jimbo and Wayne, holding hands, take deep breaths, and then pull away from each other. Johnnie stands and looks over the side as well. He tugs at Frankie, who is drooling and is face down on the floor, gripped with nausea from the sled that cuts through the clouds like a sailboat on choppy water. "Don't be a putz, Frankie." Frankie stands, though his knees wobble.

Wayne looks at his hands. "I don't even feel a chill."

Otto works his arms in a circular motion. "Works like a convection oven." They all stand and gawk at the earth below.

Wallace, sitting comfortably in his seat, reads a paper in a plane as all the passengers sleep. He glances over and sees the sled. The guys make faces at him. He rings the stewardess, and she makes her way down the aisle. "You won't believe this!" Wallace tells her and then points out the window, but the sled ducks into some thick clouds.

"What is it?" she asks him, as she glances out the window with no real concern.

"It was a sled with men on it! Out there!" She gives him a funny look and then signals toward the back as a three-year-old boy stands on his seat behind him.

"I saw it." Wallace pleads with her.

She waves over another stewardess and lays a pillow behind his head as the sled comes back into sight. "*Look*!" Wallace screams, causing some of the passengers to awaken.

"Outside! A sled!" Wallace is leaning forward and pointing now. The small child can't formulate the words but tries with a hissing "s-s-s." Passengers turn on their lights as the sled ducks out again.

"Sir, you are putting everyone in a panic," the stewardess tells him and tries to assist the child back in his seat who demands to stand and point.

"It's there!" Wallace tells them as the other stewardess enters with a couple of tablets.

"Take this," she says, but he slaps them out of her hand. "Sir, that could be considered a threat to airline security."

"Shove your airline security. I know what I saw." The stewardess backs off. The boy behind them jumps up and down on the seat, pointing outside, but the stewardess slams the window shut and turns off the light. "We'll deal with this when we touch down."

Wallace stares out the window as the boy behind him repeats "Santa." The dad leans over the seat toward Wallace. "I don't know what you've done, but my son has never attempted a word in his life." Wallace, uninterested, waves him off and drinks his miniature bottle of vodka while watching outside and muttering under his breath, "Don't know what games you are playing, Roy, but I'll get you."

Life in the North Pole

A small set of lights comes into view from the earth below. Sleds fly out of the North Pole, and a sled circles to let Otto's land. The elf pilot comes back on over the intercom. "Temperature is, oh, about twenty below, moderate humidity. Prepare for landing, and, uh, welcome to the North Pole." An elf in heavy snow gear signals the sled with two red light beams. Another elf runs to the left with a bucket of oats, and the lead reindeer quickly follows. They hit a small runway as another sled is prepared for takeoff. *Sparks* fly from the sliding hoofs.

An elf newscaster sits at the desk. "And in other news, we had some visitors from ..." He studies them as Wayne steps out of the sled and studies his surroundings and then belts out. "American workers are here ... home of the free, baby!" Expecting Finnish toymakers, the elf newscaster looks back over his notes and through a couple of other pages. "America? And in other news ..."

Elves stand glued to the television in a local tavern, and they're immediately hit with a groin shot of the guys stepping off the sled. The elf cameraman works quickly to adjust the stand. The guys wave at the elf onlookers like they were celebrities.

The elf reporter adjusts his tie and looks into the camera. "A change has obviously been made as eight American factory workers have been sent to replace ailing employees."

Wayne grabs the little microphone from him. "Hold on to your daughters! Rock and roll!" He gives a rock-and-roll sign and makes faces into the camera.

Jimbo gives the "rabbit ears" sign behind the reporter and leans down. "Hello, North Pole!" He gives a big thumbs up. The elf reporter squares up with Roy, who is all business and tries to maneuver around him, but the reporter demands answers. "Do you think that you can effectively fill in for the elves?" Roy continues to walk as Frankie is doubled over and about to get sick. Roy leans down. "We came here to do a job. No more comments." Roy waves off the cameraman. Frankie staggers behind them and falls to the ground. The elf reporter holds the microphone down to Frankie but only gets a weak whimper. He squares back up with the camera. "You heard it here first, folks. Back to the station."

One elf turns to another in the bunk room as they watch elf-vision. "These are our replacements?" A brief moment of silence, and then laughter and knee slapping break out amongst all of the elves.

An elf taxi driver with a cigar and bushy hair pulls up in a yellow sled until Otto waves him off. "Beat it!" Otto turns to the guys. "You won't mix with the locals. Only the chosen few are allowed on Santa's property."

A shuttle sled pulls up for the guys. Small sleds with elves eager for a destination pass by them. An elf in a sled sees the guys and almost hits the elf officer conducting traffic, causing him to spill the hot chocolate he holds with his free hand. The elf officer glances over and almost swallows his whistle, and other elves begin to notice them. An elf putting up lights slips and falls down a roof and onto a cart, causing it to collapse.

"Don't mind them. They just never saw anyone taller than four feet," the elf taxi driver tells them. Otto leans close to the men. "Don't say anything, and don't ask for anything when you see the Big Man."

"Big Man?" Crane asks.

"Santa." Otto reminds him.

"*Santa Claus?*" Jimbo screams out, and the elf shuttle driver swerves but corrects himself in a hurry. "That's exactly what I'm talking about." Otto moans.

A tall fence surrounds the workshop. Otto flashes a badge to a security elf, who waves him on. Otto brazenly turns back at the guys. "Membership has its privileges."

The sled slides to a stop in front of the shop, and the elf shuttle driver runs around to get their door. The group makes its way up a long walkway lined with ice sculptures of Santa in different poses and stops at a seven-foot-tall toy soldier who waves them on with this stiff, wooden arm. Roy is bumped on the ankle and looks down to see a tiny baby reindeer with a flickering red nose trying to stand up and walk. He leans down and helps it up on its wobbly, skinny legs. The mother makes two long leaps and lands in front of Roy, spraying his face with snow and Wayne laughing. Roy backs away as she nudges her baby along. Otto waves him to the front door.

They stand in front of an enormous oak door with huge profiles of elves chiseled in it that dwarfs them all. Otto grabs the knocker that hangs waist level to the men and knocks three times. The guys take a step back but strain to see inside. Rustling can be heard and then nothing. Johnnie begins to scratch himself, and Roy slaps his hand away and then straightens up his hair, encouraging the others to follow suit.

The door creaks as it slowly opens. They all look down as a mouse looks straight ahead and almost shut the door until he looks up. He runs back inside and Otto pulls the door open for the group.

"Come on inside."

Machines with long arms churn and rumble. Pipes wind around the room. A toy plane circles above them, and Otto points at it. "Watch your head."

Rowdy walks in with a few of his elves and they exchange glares. Santa walks down a few steps as Roy steps forward and extends a hearty handshake. "You must be Santa."

Santa looks up but then misses the last step and falls. Santa looks up as the men look down on him. Santa looks over at Otto, who tries to sneak out. "Who are these people?"

Roy offers a hand. "Roy Hoskins."

"Hubcap King of the Midwest," Wayne spouts off. Roy tries to pull Santa up but has no luck, and the others go to assist him. They heave him up and Santa yells at Otto who is almost out the door. "These aren't the men I sent for."

Roy offers a handshake. "I want to thank you for allowing us." Santa cuts him off and looks back at Otto.

"These are not the men I sent you for, Otto!"

Back in Finland, eight Finnish men, all blond and the same height, stand side by side at the door waiting with suitcases. They look up at the sky and then at each other.

Otto marches across the floor. "These guys are factory workers. Plus, how the heck am I—"

"—Otto!" Santa screams out.

"It was Bristo's idea. Otto looks around. "Oh, boy."

"You left Bristo?" Santa's face becomes red as Otto is once again looking for the door.

Meanwhile, in the bowling alley, Bristo sits in the corner of the bar, holding his briefcase to his chest. The bartender turns off the lights and looks back at Bristo.

"Come on." Bristo hops off the stool and walks out with him.

Back in the toy shop, Johnnie plays with a toy race car. Santa talks to him through his teeth and knows that he immediately doesn't like these guys. "Put…that…down…" Johnnie puts the toy down and moves closer to the others. Santa squares up with Roz and studies her up and down.

Roz jabs Santa in the stomach, and he quickly doubles over in pain. "Don't miss too many meals, do ya?" She continues. "Roz Kelly, darn glad to meet ya."

Santa regains his composure and pulls a couple of metal ornaments out and rotates them in his palm to ease the tension. He smiles and counts to himself. "One potato, two potato…" Santa extends a handshake and bows to Roz. "Nice to meet you, Roz Kelly. A tough woman with sensitive needs." Santa puts the ornaments in his pocket and rubs out the soreness in his ribs.

"Speak for yourself," Roz tells him as she walks away, studying the equipment until suddenly the lights go out, leaving the room in darkness.

Santa screams, "Don't move!"

The lights go back on and Frankie throws his hands up. "Sorry."

Santa paces in front of the guys. "We do need workers, and it looks like you guys are it…for now."

"What do we get paid?" Sutter belts out as the guys all look toward Santa except Roz, who is digging through their garbage. Santa squares up in front of Sutter. "Haven't changed since childhood, I see." He puts his hand on Sutter's shoulder, but Sutter pushes him away. "Nobody touches the Sutter."

Sutter walks to the opposite corner of the room and lights up a cigarette. An elf jumps and tries to grab the cigarette unsuccessfully. Santa walks to Johnnie and Frankie. "Two devoted brothers who lost their mother when they were very young. If I remembered correctly, you two fought like cats and dogs."

"Ended up in the pen." Frankie chimes in but is quickly punched in the arm by Johnnie.

"You don't tell Santa that, stupid." Frankie grabs Johnnie in a headlock.

Santa struggles to remember while pointing at Johnnie. "You wanted the green motorcycle and (pointing at Frankie) you the red."

Frankie lets go and jumps in front of Santa. "I wanted the green." Johnnie nudges him out of the way. "Me, the red," Johnnie tells him.

Santa looks back at Jimbo, and Frankie punches Johnnie in the chin, buckling his knees and dropping him to the floor. Santa walks to Jimbo. "A strong reliable man who once was trapped inside a child's body. Maybe it's time to be the child inside the man's body."

Jimbo looks at the others. "I think you've got the wrong guy."

"Just don't be the child on company time." Santa walks to Crane and then stands over him as he wilts. "Crane, my friend. Everyone's friend. You're always doing for others. This time if you receive a gift, keep it for yourself."

Crane stands up straight, and Roy puts his hand on Crane's shoulder. Santa takes a step back, but is not quite finished with Crane. "Hygiene was never your strong point." Santa stops in front of Roy, and Roy can see a twinkle in his eye as he sizes him up. "And Roy … Roy Hoskins." Santa places his hand on Roy's shoulder. Roy looks him squarely in the eye. "A man in search of his own island."

"Yeah, the Virgin Islands," Wayne says, as he is the only one to find this humorous.

"I'll get to you," Santa tells Wayne.

"Just trying to lighten the mood." Wayne stands up straight and smiles as he eagerly awaits his turn.

"Thank you." Santa moves back to address the whole group. "I'm glad you're here, and we have a lot of work to do."

Wayne looks at the guys in disbelief. "What about my fortune? Or prophecy or whatever?"

Santa claps his hands. "Listen up! We don't have a lot of time. We need to."

"Sleep." Sutter deadpans.

Frankie studies a small hammer, and then uses it as a back scratcher.

"We have a lot of work to do!" Santa yells at them and then to Otto. "Get Bristo!"

Mrs. Claus walks out into the room with cookies. "It is so nice you men could join us." She is followed by female elves that bring milk jugs out.

Santa steps in front of Roy. "This is a job that we perform until completed. No breaks. No slacking."

"Wait a minute, Supervisor Claus," Roy tells him.

"Just call me Santa."

"We're union," Jimbo yells out as a couple of terrified elves run to the opposite corner of the room, and Santa becomes flushed with anger. "Not anymore you're not, and don't give these guys any more ideas!"

Roy waves his arms to try to calm Santa down. "Thank you, Jimbo, but let me speak for the group. I mean no disrespect, but like Sutter said, we work better under a little sleep."

Rowdy jumps up on the table. "Santa said we work."

Birtnink steps in between Santa and the guys. He gives Roy a sly wink.

"Maybe it would be good for the men to get some rest and a better feel for the place."

Rowdy takes a stepladder and goes nose to nose with Roy. "I'm in charge here and say we work." Roy offers a hand to Rowdy to help him off the table, but he slaps it away.

Santa walks back to his room. "Corky. Show these men to their room."

"Room?" Wayne asks.

Airport Security

Wallace stands in front of four armed guards in the airport who fight the urge to smack him. "Don't you idiots have any idea of what that was?" Wallace asks.

An officer begins to put handcuffs on him as another officer steps in front of Wallace holding a manual. "You will not use that language nor that tone."

"What language?" Wallace struggles to break free as a security officer tries to click the handcuffs on his wrist but slips to his knees. The other officer reads out of the manual.

"You will be detained for up to up to forty-eight hours," he tells Wallace, who backs into the counter to make it more difficult to close the handcuffs.

"There is a sled up there! Check the monitors or something!" Wallace tells them. "Are you not going to at least investigate this, or is that reserved for real cops?" He bumps the officer away and runs toward the door.

They all lunge at him and Wallace ducks under them and starts to run but is grabbed, and his jacket tears. "Not the jacket," he whines and then shoves them and runs out in the airport food court area. A guard shoots his gun, causing screaming people to duck for cover. One of the guards smacks the other. "What are you doing?" They take off after Wallace, who is sliding down an escalator.

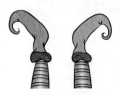

Getting Acquainted

Roy and his workers, Corky and Rowdy, all stand silent as elevator Christmas music plays.

"Had a doozy of a snowstorm today." Corky fidgets as usual and continues. "Maybe it was yesterday."

They all look straight ahead until a mouse straightens his hat and then punches the floor button. The elevator struggles with the weight, and Frankie is once again clutching the side turning a light shade of green. It slowly moves upward and then comes to a halt. The mouse stands straight with his arms at his side until he announces in a squeaky voice, "Third floor." They exit the elevator.

Corky leads the group down a hallway lined with portraits of distinguished elves. He points at the pictures. "Head elves … all of them."

A hand reaches out of the painting and grabs Johnnie's cap. Johnnie stops, goes back, flexes, and the portrait spits the cap back out. "That's what I'm talking about." A wooden mallet is tossed out and hits Johnnie in the face. Johnnie shakes his fist at the picture. Frankie licks the licorice railing and Johnnie smacks him. "C'mon."

Johnnie and Frankie bump their heads as they walk through the tiny door of their large bunk room.

Corky jumps on a forty-foot wide bed and points. "If you need to use the bathroom, it's over there. Hungry?

Eat the furniture. Marital advice? Summon the snow-man outside."

"There's a name for eight guys who sleep together," Sutter tells them, but they don't pay him any attention.

"Hey, uh, Fruitcake." Frankie asks Corky, as he is pulling out the blanket for the group. "About the sleeping arrangements." Frankie turns to Roy.

"Pick a spot." Roy tells him as he lays out his shirt.

"I'll take the front." Frankie responds and Johnnie follows him.

Roy drops on the bed. Sutter tosses his bag down and goes to the opposite side of the bed. "We are in the North Pole. Can you believe what is going on?" Jimbo excitedly runs around the room. "Somebody pinch me." Jimbo bounces on the bed and waves at the others to join him. "C'mon, guys. When in Rome!"

"Let's get a good night's—" Roy asks him, but it's too late. *Whack*! Roy is hit upside the head with a pillow, and Jimbo playfully taunts him. "C'mon! Give me your best shot."

Wayne jumps on the bed. "*We are in the North Pole!*"

Wayne and Jimbo bounce on the bed together as Roz sets up a spot on the floor and pulls out her own blanket.

"I'll wait over here," Johnnie says as he moves toward Roz, who glares at him. He cautiously moves away, and she lays down a small pillow from her jacket.

Jimbo bounces too high and hits the ceiling, sending him plummeting back down like a limp sack of potatoes.

Candy drops out like a piñata all over his unconscious body, and the guys run to pick the candy off his back. Wayne grabs a pillow case and shoves candy in it as Roz licks on a lollipop. Johnnie drapes his belongings over a chair. He takes a bite out of the coffee table.

"Coffee cake?" He grabs more. Roy admires the group until he pulls out a picture of Sam, and the joy is gone. Sorrow shrouds his face. He shuffles in under the covers. "Let's get some sleep. We've got a long day tomorrow."

The others climb in bed and pull the covers up as light Christmas music plays and the notes dance above them. Frankie curls up and giggles to himself as Johnnie is already asleep and snoring with a large chocolate stain around his mouth. The guys are spread out across the room, feet hanging everywhere.

Sutter lays awake and stares at the wall. He holds a small toy soldier in his hand and then *snap*! It breaks between his fingers.

First Day on the Job

Light moves across the floor through a multicolored, stained glass window as the sun rises. The light makes its way across the floor, over a table, creeps around a sleeping elf and hits the clock on the wall squarely in the face. The clock awakens and stretches its arms. Rowdy stands in front of the bed and pulls out a trumpet. He collects as much air as his inflated cheeks will fit and forces as much noise out of the trumpet as possible. He drops it to his side. "Rise and shine, folks. We've got lots of work to do." They slowly roll out of bed.

Rowdy leads the group down the hall. Johnnie rubs his eyes and then pulls his stocking cap over them as Christmas music plays. "Too early for this!" Johnnie tells them.

"I could really use a cup of coffee and a smoke." Frankie pleads with Roy, who shakes his head "no."

Rowdy walks down a hall with his back to them. "I was told to give you guys the tour, then break you into groups." Rowdy opens the door for the guys. "This is where dreams become a reality." The room is filled with blinking lights and a round orb in the middle.

Jimbo leans closer to it and Rowdy stops him. The group crowds around. Inside the orb a small boy, too short to play football but idolizing his local high school heroes, can be seen praying in front of his bed. "And a football," the boy whispers.

Johnnie steps toward the orb and yells at the child. "Don't be a putz! Ask for a gold chain!"

Frankie adds, "Or a motorcycle." Johnnie and Frankie crowd around the orb.

They yell together as they huddle over the orb. "Ask for a Harley! Harley! Do it!" They are almost touching the orb when Rowdy shoves them back before they get too close. Inside the little boy's room, a beam of light comes through the window and a hologram of Johnnie's elongated nose stretches out before him. The boy runs out of the room screaming.

Rowdy walks back out and signals them to follow. Wayne grabs Rowdy. "When do we get breakfast?"

"No time for breakfast." Rowdy waits for them then walks down the hall. Frankie looks back and shuffles around Roz and starts walking back. The guys walk by an elf room where a couple of elves put on their uniforms and look in a mirror to make sure they look appropriate for the shop. Rowdy walks to one and looks him up and down and then gives him the look of approval, then nods for him to leave. "Preparation," Rowdy tells them and then to the elf tailor, "Let's make sure these are regulation." Sitting in the back of the room and casually sitting in a chair, an elf stylist gives Otto a manicure on his long, jagged fingernails. He takes a swig off his North Pole moonshine. "You guys are still here! Ha! This is great." He holds up a flask, laughs, and begins to sing some Sinatra, crooning, "Fly me to the moon."

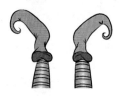

Back in the Orb Room

Frankie, looking in all directions, walks to the orb with his hands out. "I want a Harley, I want a Harley, I want..." Frankie places his hands on the orb, and his hair shoots straight up. He can't let go of the orb, and his body wildly convulses.

Rowdy stands before the guys in the hallway. "About the orb. It is set on a high electrical current so that satellites can pick it up." Frankie finally pulls himself away. Smoke rolls off his hair. He falls backwards and moans.

A wall-size computer spits out long lists of children's names. Rowdy walks up to a list and holds it out in front of the guys. "We know what every child is doing. They are all accounted for." Rowdy checks the list and then signals an elf over and whispers something to him. The elf nods and inputs the information into a computer the size of the wall. Rowdy walks out and signals for them to follow him.

"Frankie?" Johnnie looks around for Frankie and then walks to the list unnoticed as the others walk down the hall. He pulls out a lighter and searches the list. He lights it up.

"Gonna take care of ya, little Tony." He runs to another list and accidentally catches it on fire. It falls and hits another list. "Hey, uh, Frankie? Need a little help here." Small fires sprout up and Johnnie sneaks out.

Birtnink observes from another room unnoticed as he peers around the corner and smiles to himself.

Back in the hallway, Rowdy leads the way when Jimbo stops at a bell on the wall and toys with it, but Rowdy tries to stop him. "Does an angel get his wings?" Jimbo rings the bell, and elves in white chef jackets line the hall. Rowdy puts up his arm and signals to the workers. "False alarm, everyone." They quickly disperse. Rowdy looks back at Jimbo. "Please do not touch anything."

Rowdy sniffs the air, and the fire alarm goes off. He looks back at the guys, who throw up their arms. Roy looks over the group and drops his head as Frankie and Johnny quickly join them. Rowdy waves them along.

Inside the huge warehouse, toys are stacked on rows and rows of racks that lead off into the distance and upward. Elf firemen run down the hall with a long hose, almost knocking Crane down, who rushes to get out of the hallway.

"Wonder what that could be, Frankie?" Johnnie nudges Frankie. "No idea, Johnnie." Frankie tries to smash down his hair and Johnnie tries to put out the small flames on his butt.

Rowdy walks besides the huge toy rack. "Toys are divided up into different columns." He walks and points. "Educational, board games, puzzles, popular, dolls, stuffed animals, and live animation games."

Roy looks closer. "Now I gotta know. Live animation?"

"It's not quite ready. I'll tell ya, if you can come up with a toy...the toy, then you would live comfortably for the rest of your life." Rowdy speaks aloud to himself. "It's been awhile. I sort of like these critters." He turns to the group. "Gather 'round." Rowdy has them circle around him and a box that rattles and then sits still. They eagerly watch what awaits them.

"Ready?" Rowdy asks, looking back at them as they are hunched over the top. He opens the lid and animated characters hop out and run in different directions. Crane scoops up an animated rabbit that whacks him in the face with its long ear. "What's up, thilly?" It hops and goes bouncing away as Crane almost falls to his knees reaching for it. "Darn."

A fat, lime green cuddly monster hops, out and Roy sweeps him up in his arms. It shouts out to Roy. "Howdy, twin!"

An animated teddy bear lands a big kiss on Roz then winks.

"Well, aren't you a darling," Roz tells the teddy bear who answers. "Single?"

The guys run around the warehouse picking up animated characters.

The guys and Rowdy crowd in front of long, wavy cylinders with sparkling colors that swirl to the top and bubbles out the end. They stand about twenty-feet high and have a tulip opening at the top. "Sort of like this one." Rowdy tosses a ball up, and the cylinder droops down, allowing the ball to go in the top and make its way to the bottom. The ball rolls out the bottom and to their feet. The cylinder moves like a dog waiting to fetch a bone. "These are great." Rowdy tells them as he scoops up the ball and tosses it again. "Especially for children who can't toss it." Rowdy is abruptly cut off by a cylinder that pops him on the head. "We thought about chopping them in half because they droop a little too much."

The cylinders straighten up. Rowdy waves the group to follow him.

Finally ... the Toy Shop

Corky holds up red uniforms with white trim. "Ain't gonna happen," Sutter tells him, nodding his head. Sutter picks a uniform up, laughs at it, and then tosses it aside.

"It's the rules." Corky tells them.

"You *know* what you can do with your rules." Sutter walks to one of the tables.

Rowdy walks in wearing a jacket. Wayne, looking over an outfit, kneels down to Rowdy and taunts him. "Those little outfits are so cute."

Rowdy grabs a Christmas wreath and signals for Wayne to move closer. Wayne continues taunting him. "Just like a little Hawaiian." Wayne smiles as Rowdy slams it over his shoulder like a hockey player, pulling over a jersey and punches him across the chin.

Rowdy does a couple of quick scissor kicks, knocking Wayne to the ground.

"Never mock my world." Rowdy starts to bite Wayne's ear when Santa walks in.

"Having fun, Rowdy?" Santa stands at the entrance. Rowdy hops up.

A mouse on the table adjusts his glasses, then wipes his tiny forehead off with a rag and goes back to work on a stuffed animal. An elf hammers a wheel on a wagon.

"Where do you want us?" Roy asks Santa.

"I need these toys by Friday!" Santa tells them. "Nobody

moves until then. *And no breaks!*" Santa begins to stomp out when Roy calls out to him. "How about just a little respect?"

Santa starts in again. "Respect? I lost ninety percent of my workforce." Santa makes his way toward Roy, who stands his ground.

"Hey, you invited us here." Roy turns back to Santa.

"No, I didn't." Santa fires back, and Roy goes back to finding work for himself.

Santa points at Rowdy. "I want a full report from you by the end of the day." Santa storms out of the shop and into his room.

"How many ya need of whatever?" Frankie asks Corky.

"I think six hundred..." Frankie shrugs until he finishes. "... seventy-two thousand and four... maybe five." Frankie drops his head, exposing a bald patch from the fire on his head. Rowdy hands out small hammers. Tall speakers dance to the Christmas music that plays in the far corner of the shop. Rowdy gives a smug smile to the group. "Welcome to Santa's workshop."

Crane fumbles with a wheel at the assembly line as Corky looks on unimpressed. Corky turns a lever and stops the line to allow Crane to catch up.

Jimbo stands at a small wooden table, trying to get a grip on a small wrench. He assembles a toy wagon and glances over at the mouse, who has finished four. Rowdy shows a few of his elves to a table with wood products. One of Santa's elves intentionally drops his hammer and stares at Wayne. The elf throws down his tools. "I'm not working alongside your scabs." He points at Roy's group. "Or those overgrown morons." "You want me to tell Santa what you guys are really up to?" Rowdy tells him as he shoves a hammer in the other elf's chest.

Roz stocks items in the warehouse and decides to

look in the animation box. A small furball jumps out and she runs after it. "I don't have time for this!" she hollers.

Everyone seems to know their job at the moment, and they focus on work in the shop except for Sutter, who takes a break. Crane stands at the assembly line and fumbles with a toy until an elf hits the off button. He shows Crane how to assemble an arm on a robot. Roy stands at a table and turns a wagon on its side. Frankie watches the clock as Johnnie slaps himself to stay awake. Jimbo dances to Christmas music in the corner of the room when Rowdy signals him back over. An alarm goes off, and Corky looks up as if they are going to be bombed. "Trolls!" Rowdy looks back at the men and then grabs his hammer and a wrench. "Bullies. I knew they would come but not this soon." Rowdy starts for the door, but Birtnink cuts him off. "I would not get involved unless they are a threat to the factory."

Rowdy shoves him aside and then rolls up his sleeves. "I know you wouldn't."

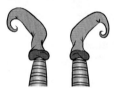

Misunderstood Trolls

Outside, seven-foot-tall furry, green trolls, about twenty of them with the stench of bad breath and body odor reaching miles away, walk through town tearing up anything in their path. Two trolls pull back a fir tree and place an elf on the end. They let it go, and he goes sailing off into the distance and lands in a snow bank.

Three trolls play football with a local elf, making him the football. Elf police officers surround a troll. It growls and they run. There's a feeling of pure panic in the streets of the North Pole as elves scramble to get as far away as possible. Shops close and the windows are slammed shut. Korean elves stand on the rooftop of a grocery store, aiming popguns at any troll who dares to come close. A troll chews on a fender, and it drops out of his mouth as he looks up. All the trolls stop what they are doing and shift their focus. Rowdy walks to the opposite side of the fence with the guys close behind him. An elf security guard hides in his booth. A troll pulls out a large fence post as the others boldly make their way toward the shop.

"They're trying to get to the toy shop!" Corky calls out to the guys, who are already on the opposite side of the fence and braced for a fight. Rowdy stands his ground and points at the trolls, giving them an ultimatum. "I'm gonna give you *girls* one opportunity to leave the premises."

The trolls growl. Slime drips from their mouths. One of them moves closer and spits slime that hits Sutter's work boots. Sutter observes the slime and looks up at the troll. "You shouldn't have done that…you really shouldn't have done that."

Rowdy runs forward, but Sutter holds out his arm. "This one is mine." Sutter pops his knuckles and punches the troll across the chin, knocking him backwards.

The other trolls run toward them and Frankie steps forward, cracking his knuckles. "Ya think he might need some help?" Elves come out of hiding and watch from windows and rooftops. Jimbo stretches his arms. "Why not?" Jimbo bear hugs a troll and drops him.

Johnnie and Frankie throw punches in a troll's gut, causing him to wallow in pain and stumble back. Wayne pokes a troll in the eyes, then punches it across the jaw. It swings back, and Wayne grabs it around the waist and tosses it on the ground. Roz is squared up with two of them. "You know, where I come from, women don't take that crap!"

She throws elbows to both but they are unfazed. "Didn't work, huh?"

She takes a skillet out of her jacket pocket and whacks both of them. Rowdy wrestles with one until the troll throws him aside, but he dives back in and swings as high as he can before getting knocked back again. Jimbo grabs the troll, and Rowdy jumps back in. "I can handle him." Jimbo backs off as he is grabbed behind by a troll and dropped to the ground. They wrestle on the ground, and Jimbo gains control and gets on top. He wets his finger and thinking that might not have much impact, head butts the troll, who tries to get to its knees.

The guys work over the trolls and the trolls back off.

The trolls, bruised and beaten, walk back hanging their heads.

A sullen troll walks by a terrified elf, picks up the elf's hat, and hands it back to him.

An elf shop owner walks to Sutter. "Thank you." Sutter doesn't acknowledge and walks back to the shop.

The guys walk back inside and move to their work stations. Roy stops at the entrance and slaps the seven-foot-tall toy soldier on the shoulder while mocking him. "Thanks for all the help."

"Don't mention it."

Rowdy walks next to Roy. "Believe it or not, they used to be our friends."

Sutter grabs an elf uniform and wipes off his boot as he listens. Roy takes his small hammer and carries it with him to a table. "I can understand why they're not invited to any parties." Roy looks back at Johnnie and Frankie, who give each other high-fives.

Rowdy continues. "They were good workers until the higher-ups decided to replace them with a couple of forklifts. They tried to picket but realized they couldn't spell, at least not that well, decided there was no use for 'em and decided to retreat back in the caves, only coming out occasionally to intimidate us but your guys took care of that."

"Let's get back to work, you two." Roy tells Frankie and Johnnie, then grabs a toy plane and slides the wings in place.

Rowdy stands next to Roz and Crane. "Simple. There is really nothing to it." Crane shrugs, looks over the line, and picks up a toy leg. "Looks simple enough."

Rowdy slaps him on the back. "Just try to keep up." Toy parts move swiftly down the conveyer belt. Crane tries to grab the parts but fumbles them, dropping one on the ground. He reaches down to grab it but another is headed his way. He reaches for the one on the line and is able to get a grip on it when another heads his way.

Birtnink jumps in between them. "Might have to try you at something else."

"They're gonna fire me," a worried and stressed Crane tells an uninterested Roz.

"Probably." She takes the toy and puts a leg on it and lays it on the line. Things are moving rather smoothly as Rowdy takes a toy and tosses it to one of his worker elves, who hands to another to make the final touches on it. Jimbo drops a toy in the box and rings a bell. Sutter looks back. "Are we supposed to ring the bell every time we finish a toy?"

"Sorta thought of that on my own." Jimbo says as he finished another and leans over to ring the bell, but Rowdy is there to stop him.

"No bell . . . and no thinking on your own!"

Santa practices his tip-toeing with a mouse in his room. The mouse looks up, and Santa is visually frustrated and turning red. "I can't get any quieter, and I don't plan on dieting." Santa lifts his foot when Roy burst in the room and Santa jumps. Crunch! "I have an idea for the—" Roy and Santa slowly look down. Santa looks closer. "Oh, no."

"I, uh, got an idea to speed up, uh, production, Mr. Claus." Roy says, but Santa trembles with anger at Roy's site. "Ya mind knocking next time? Medic!" Santa leans down.

"Maybe I should come back a little later." Roy slips back out the door.

Jimbo applies a little oil to a jack-in-the-box. He cranks its handle, but it won't open until Corky creeps up close to it and gently speaks at the box. "C'mon, little buddy. I want to give you a treat." Corky pulls his sleeve back as it opens and then abruptly shuts. Corky prepares himself again as it slowly opens. Tiny eyes are visible amongst the darkness in the box, and he grabs the tiny Jack out of the box. Corky throws it in a large box with others. He reaches in the box as miniature Jacks try to resist.

"Please, no. The endless bobbing up and down." The Jack cries out, but Corky pulls him out and stuffs him in the box and gives Jimbo a tough look. "Not too glamorous, huh?"

Jimbo looks into the empty box. "No. Not really."

We'll save these guys for the new boxes." Corky reaches into another box and Jimbo sneaks away.

Roz stops and sits on a table. She takes off a dirty sock and rubs her feet. An elf working at the table becomes unstable on his feet from the pungent odor until Rowdy catches him and sets him down safely. Rowdy glares at her and she puts her sock back on. "I got ya, ya pointy-eared pygmy."

Jimbo carries an arm full of wooden parts and then drops them. "Isn't it about break time?"

"Not like this!" Birtnink says to one of Rowdy's workers. He holds a teddy bear with the stuffing coming out the side. "I knew this would not work out!"

Rowdy goes nose-to-nose with Birtnink. "Lay off my elf!"

"Remember, this is only temporary." Birtnink looks over the floor and laughs to himself before walking off. "I'll be back later to check on *your* crew."

Rowdy walks to Roy and pulls him aside. The others watch them as Rowdy leads Roy to the corner of the room and whispers to him. "Your boy Crane is a little slow."

Roy looks back and makes eye contact with Crane, who knows they are talking about him. "He's not familiar with your system," Roy explains to him.

"I'm gonna try him out in another area."

Roy slaps Rowdy on the shoulder and the music plays. "Can you do something about this music?"

Down in an elf mine shaft, an elf miner hands Crane a pick axe. The elf miner speaks in a deep, gruff voice as a small amount of soot blows out with every syllable. "Take a (cough) small amount." He grabs a small box. "And drop the coal in like so." Crane observes his surroundings. "Got it?" The elf miner coughs, then starts to gag. He wipes his mouth with his glove. "You'll get used to it." The elf walks back down the shaft and disappears into the darkness. Crane holds the coal and looks it over.

Wayne paints the eyeball of a toy soldier as the elf looks over. "Blue, not brown."

Wayne continues to paint. "I prefer brown."

"Blue," the elf tells him, but Wayne grabs one of the toy soldiers in the elf's line and paints the eyeball. "How 'bout green?"

"Blue." The elf continues to paint his soldier, and Wayne grabs another and paints the eyeball green. The elf paints on Wayne's face. "Roy! This elf is painting on me!"

Back in the States

A sports bar is filled with fans who drink their beer and cheer for their teams except for the end of the bar. Wallace stands in front of the television when he is tapped on the shoulder. A large Chicago Bears fan with others behind him glare at Wallace. "You mind if we get back to our game?" Wallace fidgets with the remote as they crowd closer. "Trying to watch the news. Probably do you guys good to know what is going on the world." Wallace laughs to himself as he locks on a channel and sits back. "Primitive sport." He is jerked backwards.

Television—fuzzy video clip of the sled flying through the sky. Only scuffling can be heard as Wallace is being dragged away by his collar. "Not the suit."

Back at the bartender's house, he grabs his jacket and looks back at Bristo. "Just be sure to lock up if you go out." The bartender mentions as Bristo holds the over-sized remote control in his small hands and then returns his attention to the movie. The bartender observes his fascination with the movie. "You're an okay guy, Bristo."

Bristo laughs at the television and points; his short legs dangle from the couch.

"Just can't get enough, huh?" He locks the door behind him. "Lock up if you go out looking for fast women." He tells Bristo who looks back and then takes a long drink off his Coke.

Waning Interest

There is very little talk in the workshop as fatigue sets in for the workers. Johnnie watches the large round clock on the wall that reads 12:21. The second hand clicks backward and Johnnie's head drops, slamming the table and going straight to the ground. Wayne claws at himself. "Can't deal with this." An elf taps him on the shoulder and points at the toy soldier. "Blue eyes." Wayne throws the toy in the air. "Shut up with the eyes. Okay, elf?" He doesn't get a response and sticks his fingers in the paint. "Okay?" The paint runs down his clenched knuckles and then wrists.

Johnnie takes a cigarette out of the pack and points in Wayne's direction with the cigarette dangling from his fingers. "Your boy might need a break."

Wayne goes back to work on the toy soldier and Johnnie sneaks outside. Roy and Rowdy walk into Santa's room. Rowdy looks back at the workers. "Take lunch!"

Frankie walks in the elf bunkroom with a deck of cards. The elves cower back. Frankie flashes a wad of cash, and the elves move closer. "Heard I could find some action here."

A deck of cards hits the floor. "Somebody drop those?" Frankie asks as he smiles coyly at the elves who are already moving slowly off the bed toward him.

The guys eat as elves run food to them. Corky barks out to the elf servants, "Root beer!"

The guys look at Roy, who smiles. "Close enough."

Roy looks up as elves run root beers to them, and Roz slaps him on the back. "This is more like it."

Roy leans back as a root beer mug is shoved in front of him, frothing over the top. "Better than bowling night," he says with a smile. Roz downs hers and then says, "Who's keeping score?" They all laugh, and a small puff of black soot flies from Crane's mouth. Roy takes a big drink. Froth lines his mouth and almost resembles Santa as the others notice and briefly ponder to themselves. "Never felt better, guys."

Roy winks at Roz. "And girls."

She holds her root beer up. "I'm with ya."

Sutter, sitting a few feet away from the group, is solemn as opposed to the rest of the group. "Glad you feel good about yourself."

Roy looks around the room. "Where's Frankie and Johnnie?"

"Take it easy. I mean, where could they escape to?" Roz assures him.

Frankie shuts the elf room door behind him. He stops briefly, wearing only a t-shirt and cheetah underwear. He lost the rest of his clothes and money to the elves. A female elf standing in the hallway covers her eyes. "They're sharks," he tells her and then runs down the hall covering himself. "*Sharks!*" he says angrily.

Johnnie takes off his stocking cap in the transformation room and puts an elf hat on. He dances in front of the mirror. "Look at me! I'm Johnnie elf!" He does a quick draw motion and likes what he sees. He checks out his profile and winks at the mirror that winks back. Johnnie takes the hat off and places it back on the shelf. He catches his reflection in the mirror. Johnnie grabs at his ears. "Oh, my gosh." His ears come to a perfect point. He runs out of the room.

Dining

Elves with chef hats walk down the aisles with bowls of plum jam, plates of turkey, and large pastries. The guys eat vigorously when Johnnie sneaks in with his ski cap pulled over his head. Frankie rushes inside and buttons up his shirt. He sits at the table. "Where ya been, Mugshot?" he asks Johnnie as Johnnie waves over a couple of elves and then grabs food off of their trays. Roy leans over to Johnnie. "Next time you guys check with me before you decide to run off and"—Roy notices his ears, or at least one that escapes out of the top—"you've got pointy ears."

"Like Jimbo said, 'When in Rome.'" Johnnie laughs to himself and grabs his mug and tips it back, hoping nobody else will notice his transformation.

"You guys take this stuff seriously," Roz tells him. She reaches in her back pocket and takes a pair of food tongs. She grabs a roll with them.

Wayne grabs at the food. "This is more like it," he says, talking to himself. "Blue eyes? Oh, yeah, blue, that's all we've got in the North Pole…blue." Wayne looks back at the others who stop and look his way. He grabs a carrot, and they go back to eating and drinking.

Back on the Job

After the meal in the workshop, Jimbo turns the small wrench and it slips in his hand and cuts his finger. Jimbo grips his finger and Roz reaches in her jacket and hands him a Band Aid. She grabs a cigarette and Rowdy hands her a broom, but Roz shoves it back at him. "Ain't gonna happen."

Rowdy shoves is right back. "If you want to work here."

Roz tosses the broom aside as Roy quickly runs their way. "Take this job and…"

Roy hands her the broom. "Let's do what they say." She scowls at them and then jerks the broom out of Roy's hands.

Elves work around Johnnie, who sleeps in the middle of a worktable. Corky taps him on the shoulder. "Got a new assignment for you and your brother."

Bright colors of goo flow into a machine and comes out long strands of silly string. Frankie observes it and even sticks his hand in the mix, watching the colors swirl around his fingers. Frankie fills a container from a larger container. It moves rapidly, and silly string starts to spill over. "Might need a little help back here." Frankie struggles to keep up and slips and falls, allowing the colors to stream over his face. He gets to his feet and starts punching buttons and switches.

Meanwhile, an elf escorts Johnnie into a room where

taffy is being pulled by female elves. He rolls up his sleeve to expose a crude tattoo but they aren't impressed. Johnnie inspects the machinery as an elf looks on. He touches a couple of wires together when an elf approaches him. "Please don't don't do that." Johnnie waves him off.

"I can hotwire this thing if—" The elf slaps a box in his chest and Johnnie drops the wires, which snap and dance as they hit other ones. The machine starts contracting and expanding. "Must be a short in the system," Johnnie tells him.

The elves try to control it and Johnnie runs out.

Frankie tries to adjust a pressure valve in the silly string room. The valves spin and start to smoke when Frankie, frantic and clutching the side, pulls on a lever and punches buttons.

Boom! The walls shake, and Santa sits up in bed as he holds a phone to his ear. "What now?" Santa looks out the window where taffy rains down. "Mama mia!"

Mrs. Claus runs out into the bedroom. "Just a little accident." She tells Santa. Silly string rains down over the North Pole.

Elves watch outside their windows. One looks up and smirks. "I'm starting to like these guys."

An elf and his wife take in the show of falling taffy and silly string. "Ooh. Ahh."

Reindeer Ridge

Santa paces in front of the Americans without making a sound. The silence is killing them until Jimbo steps forward. "You know, you guys really know how to party." He winks at Santa, who is not amused. "Santa?"

Santa blurts out in French, "Vous êtes tous imbéciles! Vous tous." Roy steps forward. "Uh, I didn't like the way that sounded."

This time in English: "You are imbeciles! All of you!"

"Now you're getting personal," Roy tells him.

Santa continues this time, but in Spanish. "¡Usted es todos imbéciles! Todo usted." Santa stomps. "You are the head imbecile!"

Roy looks around. "I have a feeling that last one was meant for me." He looks back at the group, who all nod in agreement. Birtnink slides in next to Santa and hands him a contract. "I think the elves are feeling a little better."

Roy pokes Santa in the chest. "I'm still trying to decipher that last comment … Santa Claus." Santa bumps him backward with his belly. "So, what are you gonna do other than destroy all of my equipment, Roy?"

"You taunting me, Santa Boss?" Roy asks.

Santa laughs in his face. "No, Moonshine, it was a direct insult."

Frankie's impressed with the nickname but not to be outdone. "Nice work, Oval Office."

Roy looks at the guys and then at Santa. "If you've got a challenge, Big Boy."

They are bumping stomachs like a couple of sumo wrestlers. "I'll meet you on Reindeer's Ridge. Bring a sled." Santa rushes out.

"I'll be there," Roy tells him as Wayne paints on a toy soldier. An elf grabs the toy soldier. "Blue."

"This is blue!" Wayne screams. Wayne tips finger in the blue paint and sticks in front of the elf. "Blue! Do you understand me? *Blueeeee*!"

Roz and Roy walk side-by-side as Jimbo follows behind with Sutter. She looks at her blistered fingers and pulls some ointment from her pocket. Jimbo walks next to her and is just about enthused as she is. "This isn't quite what I expected."

Roz applies the ointment into her sore and cracking hands. "Yeah, well, at least we're getting fed."

Santa and Roy sit on sleds and dig their knuckles into the snow. Roy stretches his back and then struggles to lean forward to touch his toes. He takes two deep breaths, growls, and adjusts an elbow pad. Santa takes some snow and rubs it on his face as he stares at Roy. He spits the excess out. Roy takes snow and eats it, staring at Santa, snow dripping off the corners of his mouth. Frankie yells at Roy. "C'mon, big, tall, round!" They both look back indicating they are poised and ready. Corky walks in front of them as everyone has gathered around. He holds up a red scarf up, and the group crowds closer. Corky drops the scarf, and they push off and slide down the steep hill.

Santa and Roy zigzag and then bump each other as they travel down the hill. "You're out of your league, Roy." Santa steers the sled as it misses a branch and bounces off Roy's sled. Roy slides back over and collides with Santa, who edges him back with his shoulder.

Johnnie turns to Rowdy. "Give ya five to one odds on Santa."

"You got it." Rowdy reaches in his wallet and grabs a small bill.

Roy leans to the right, maneuvering around a tree stump. Santa hits a mogul and flies through the air until he lands on top of Roy.

Roz turns to Otto. "Is that legal?"

"Only in Austria and some parts of Arkansas," Otto tells them as he and the others lean to the right, watching the sled continue rumbling through the woods and over branches.

Santa and Roy continue down the hill as they cross the line on top of each other and then *boom*! They hit a small wood shed, splintering it. Roy rubs his head. "That hurt real bad." He clears the wood chips off of him as they continue to slide. "Stop this thing!" Santa screams as Roy is still a little dazed.

"You seem to have a lot of stress in your life." This is an odd statement for Roy, but feels it's a pretty opportune time, considering the circumstances. They slide across a frozen pond and by a penguin fishing in a hole. "Delivering Christmas? Wouldn't you?" Santa holds on tight as Roy fights to control the sled. They slide past a tombstone and sideswipe another, sending them spinning. Santa is tossed off, and Roy flips with the sled landing on top of him and banging into a pile of discarded toy wagons as it finally comes to a halt. Grabbing his leg, he limps over to Santa and assists him to his feet until the other sled still sliding, cuts them both down.

The scene is dark and ominous. A bald doll with one eye peers out at them. An owl hoots as toy legs and arms stick out of the ground. Earth shifts and moves below their feet as toy arms and legs try to find their counterparts with worms wrapped around them. Santa struggles to stand and helps Roy to his feet. "Let's get out of here."

An elf gravedigger cleans his teeth with a drumstick. "Come back when you can stay awhile." He buries his shovel into fresh patch of dirt and fills in a small hole.

Lazy and unmotivated elves napping in the toyshop go back to work as Santa is assisted inside by other elves. Roy limps to a table. Santa holds his arm, and Mrs. Claus runs out. "Is my baby hurting?"

He gives her a look of sorrow and she reaches out to

Roz, who reaches into her jacket, grabs a ruler, and hands it to Mrs. Claus. She whacks his hands continuously.

"You shouldn't be playing when there is so much work to be done!" Mrs. Claus hands the ruler back to Roz, who slides it back in her jacket. "Nice work, Mrs. Claus."

Johnnie yawns and starts to lie down on the table when *whap*! Rowdy hits him with a whip. Johnnie fires straight up. "Yeow!" He goes back to working as Rowdy circles the room. Roy limps over to Johnnie and waves him and the rest of his crew over. They follow him out the door and Rowdy chases after them. "Where are you going?"

Roy continues to walk. "I'm hungry." He limps down the hall, and Johnnie hands Rowdy his wrench. "It's not dinner yet!" Roy finds a dinner bell on the wall and rings it.

The guys sit across from the elves in the cafeteria as the mood is tense. Glares are passed back and forth as elf waitresses rush food out. An elf waiter attempts to show the specials of the day but leaves the menu with them after getting shunned. Roy bumps into Birtnink, who sits next to him when Roy demands. "Pass the salt, Elf." The guys look up as they can sense the tension between the two. Birtnink tosses it his way. "That's Birtnink to you, ya big tub of lard."

Crane grabs the salt back. "Ya callin' my buddy a big ol' tub of lard?"

Birtnink takes it back, and some of the elf workers move away from the table.

"That's what I just said, Ichabod Crane, pointy nose freak!"

"What did you call me?" Crane stands up.

Birtnink stands on the bench. "Rowdy told me you were all lazy, no good—"

"I never—" Rowdy tries to tell Crane but is quickly interrupted by Crane, who looks down on him. "He said what?" Crane is hit in the face with cake by an elf who is paid off by Birtnink to start trouble.

"You know I wouldn't insult my men." Rowdy tries to explain himself, but Birtnink grabs the beans and heaves them at him. Rowdy wipes beans from his eye and then grabs a roll. "It's on!" Roz announces as they all look at each other. Food is slung back and forth. Rowdy crawls under the table and finds Jimbo crouched on the opposite side. Rowdy still tries to explain himself to Jimbo. "You know I didn't say that."

"All you guys seem a little sneaky." Jimbo tosses the table on its side and rolls over to the next table. He reaches up and grabs a handful of food and throws it at elves on the opposite side of the room. Wayne eats and is oblivious to the food fight as he mumbles, "Blue. Blue? Blue … errr, blue."

Some of the "sick" elves watch from the side and next to the kitchen with sheer amusement.

Frankie takes one of Santa's elves and pushes his face in his plate. "Bada-bing!"

Roy and Rowdy crouch beside each other and toss food at the other elves. "Gonna show you who's boss!" Roy brags.

They fling food back and forth. An elf waitress stands still and afraid to move, holding a tray as Roz and Frankie grab food off of her tray and fling it across the room.

Wayne dabs his finger in the tray and draws an eyeball on the table. Roz and Frankie grab a tray and smash its contents of mashed potatoes in Corky's face.

Santa stomps into the room. A toy airplane flies his

way. "I have never been so mad in my ..." Otto's eyes get big and Santa notices. He looks up and *crash*! It flies into his nose. Santa can't speak, and Wayne finally looks up and breaks out into laughter. "*Haha*!"

Santa turns, and Birtnink is there to greet him with a contract. "Time we meet, Santa."

Santa is already on his way back to his room. "Roy! In my office."

Birtnink stands on the table. "You will be forced to do business with me eventually!"

"Not now, elf!"

Birtnink pleads with him. "I'm just concerned with getting Christmas to the children." Mashed potatoes drip off of Frankie's face. "I've used that one before, Cardinal Sin," says Frankie.

Santa walks into his room and Roy follows.

"You will be forced to deal with me!" Birtnink stomps his feet, slips on an orange peel, and goes flying off the table. Jimbo steps over him on the way out of the dining room.

A Bowl of Food

Roy and Santa sit at a table. Roy asks Santa, "Why did you get involved?"

"You guys are a disgrace." Santa spins a globe. His nose has a small bandage on it that flaps every time he breathes out. "Honestly. Why did you get in the business?"

"I don't condone your actions." Santa begins to loosen up and grabs a cookie but looks around to make sure it's safe.

"Lay it on me." Roy asks.

"I sent for professionals, Roy." Santa tells him. "I'm too old for this."

Roy knows there is more to the story, and it's probably been a long time since Santa has spoken to another man close to his size. "Let's hear it. What happened to encourage you to do this?"

Santa tries to remain stern but realizes that Roy can see right through him and his act.

"If you're gonna have a food fight—"

"—Next time we'll invite ya," Roy tells him as he eases back.

Santa rubs his beard. "I was a rather large kid. An orphan. Nobody could afford to feed me." He stops and looks out the window but resumes. "Had to discover my own methods."

"Petty theft?" Roy asks.

Santa points at the door. "Get out!" Roy stands, but Santa takes a deep breath and points for him to sit back down. "Just wanted to get a bite now and then." Santa grabs a photo, studies it, and then continues.

Santa reminisces. "I would have a sled waiting for me until that one time. I was climbing back up the chimney when I heard a child's voice." A young Santa climbs to the top of the chimney when the child cries out to him. He tries to make it higher up when the child cries out to him again. "That was it?" Roy asks. Young Santa goes back down the chimney.

"Had what you would call an epiphany." Santa tells him.

"Epiphany?" Roy is still not sure what he is talking about but Santa continues.

"This child holds out a broken toy. It was easy. Just had to snap a wheel back on. Then it happened." Young Santa leans down and hands the child back the toy.

"He handed me a bowl of food." Young Santa stands in the living room, trembling with the warm bowl of food in his hands. He can only stare at it until the boy hands him a spoon and trots off to bed.

Meanwhile, back in the cave, trolls pass food between themselves. Roy and Santa continue their conversation as the trolls eat their dinner.

The trolls huddle around a fire with only a few spare bones lying around. A troll picks up a rock and takes a bite out of it. The others watch as he tosses it aside, until they look away and he reaches for it.

"Santa became Santa because of a bowl of food. Steak? Lobster?" Roy jokes.

"That's not important, and please don't try to be funny. I just had never received anything . . . never fit in," Santa tells him.

The trolls sit in the cold and lonely cave, not a sound made amongst them.

"Sort of like an old friend of mine," Roy tells Santa, thinking of Sutter.

Santa runs his hands along pictures on the wall. He takes a handkerchief and wipes one off that shows him at the bottom of a dog pile with laughing and smiling elves. "It's not a great story but, you know." Santa places the picture back on the wall.

"Funny how an innocent child can change your life with one unselfish act."

"Seems to me you were the considerate one," Roy tells Santa and then continues.

"It's been awhile since you've talked to anyone over four feet tall."

"Other than my wife, yes." Roy walks around the room looking at the floor. "I think your men would respect you more if you rolled up the sleeves and got on the floor with them."

"You worry about your men, and I'll worry about mine." Santa tells Roy.

"And you seem to not want the experts to do their job," Roy tells Santa, trying to get a reaction out of him but Santa can only respond in a weak tone while looking at the floor. "Maybe it's time I let someone else take over." Santa checks his watch and takes a deep breath. "I'm sorry Roy. I want your men out tomorrow evening."

"Still have a job to finish. A few more days."

Birtnink, listening behind the door, bursts in and Roy gets up from the chair and starts for the door. "Did I interrupt something?"

Roy brushes him aside. "Only one Santa."

Roy walks through the dark shop and sees a figure hunched over a table. He walks to it and sees that the figure is holding a paintbrush, and it's Wayne. Roy puts his hand on Wayne's back "Time to pack it in, Wayne."

Wayne abruptly turns; his wild eyes are outlined in blue. "*I'm not finished!*" Wayne quickly continues painting. Roy picks up his tools. "Come to the room when you're ready." Roy walks out of the room. The clock, eyes outlined in blue, goes to sleep and snores. The lights go out.

All the guys lay in the bed snoring except for Sutter, who throws his jacket on and walks out but bumps into Crane, black-faced. "Where are you going?" Crane asks.

"Out." Sutter walks out and down the hall.

Elves lay in bed in the bunkroom and watch "Santa's Funniest Bloopers" videos. One elf turns to another. "Maybe we should go back to work."

The other elf watches the bloopers but whispers back, "Birtnink said he is close to negotiations."

The television shows different shots of Santa accompanied by elf laughter.

Santa slides off a roof and on top of garbage cans. Lights go on and Santa runs around the house.

Santa pulls on a garage door. The veins in his neck bulge as he struggles with it. It finally goes up and takes him with it. Only his convulsing feet are visible as they hang out the top of the garage door.

The elf smacks the other trying to get his attention. "I mean, c'mon."

Santa is chased by wild dogs in the video and runs down a street, ducking into a back alley.

"It's our job," the elf tells him and this time is accompanied by, "Shhhh" from some of the other elves.

Santa is chased down a street by police, who fire off a couple of rounds. The elves are howling with laughter.

The other elf looks his way. "Let those guys do the

work." He looks back at the television and laughs with the others.

Wallace's Struggles

Wallace, bruised and beaten from the sports bar, hands the woman at the counter of a car rental agency his credit card as he is destined to make it back to Detroit. She holds it and looks back up at Wallace, who tears a strand off his jacket and throws it away. He observes the improvement with satisfaction as she makes a phone call. She crouches down as he struggles to see out of a swollen eye. Wallace notices and reaches down. "Why don't you just give me back my card?" he asks her.

She swings the phone at him, and Wallace runs out but catches his jacket on the door. "Not the jacket."

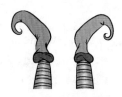

Sutter Sheds His Skin

Sutter walks through the marketplace consisting of vegetables and fish carts. A polar bear wraps a salmon tightly in newspaper as he sits next to his cart. He gives Sutter a nod and then offers the salmon but no response.

The polar bear holds the salmon out to him. "Broiled salmon with some Hollandaise sauce smothered in garlic butter can really entice the flavor." This also elicits no response to the polar bear, who watches Sutter walk away in no particular direction with no destination. The polar bear hands it to an elf. "Whateva."

Elves stop and stare. Sutter growls at them. An elf child begins to follow him with a gift but the polar bear, understanding the pain in Sutter's eyes, waves him off. The narrow road is just wide enough for Sutter as sleds move with caution past him on the shoulder. Sutter throws a punch in the air, possibly trying to thrust away the grief, resentment, and jealousy he carries with him.

Two Days Left

Santa paces in his room holding a phone to his ear. "A red one … Yes … Parts? The galvanized metal … I'll call ya back on the camper."

The workshop is almost bare, and the toys slowly trickle out of the machine. The clock on the wall sleeps, its arms hang limply down. Jimbo nudges Corky and then snorts. "Do you have to breathe so loud?"

"Do you mind keeping up with the rest of us?" Corky hisses at Jimbo and then throws his hammer down and starts to walk off, but Jimbo trips him. Corky pops right back up. "You meant to do that."

"Of course I did," Jimbo states.

Corky pokes Jimbo in the eye, and Jimbo grabs Corky by the back of his jacket, lifting him off the ground. Roy moves in quickly to break them up and then looks around the room. "Anybody seen Sutter?" Jimbo maneuvers around Roy. "Who cares? I mean, heck, he walked out on us." Jimbo smacks Corky in the face and Roy walks out. Corky slaps Jimbo back and runs. "You better run!" Jimbo turns, picks up his tools and is hit in the back of the head by a candy cane as Corky taunts him from the door, making faces. Roy grabs his jacket and Roz glances up. "He walked out on us, Roy. Let him go."

Roy shoves toys off of a table while an elf watches. "You guys weren't cut out for this."

Roy rushes out, and the elf picks up the toys. "Don't bother, I've got it."

Roy walks outside and immediately covers up from the cold. The elf security guard opens the gate for Roy. Roy walks along a street back to the landing strip. He looks in all directions. "Sutter!" Roy walks toward a sled hanger and looks around.

He walks in as two overalls-wearing, dirty elf mechanics repair a sled. "How's she running?" Roy asks them.

The two mumbling elf mechanics look up but continue working on the side of the sled, placing different panels on it. One stands back as the sled fires up and roars loudly. One greasy elf mechanic wipes his hands with a rag. "Sonofagun got little drag off takeoff, thinkn' shortin' wing, bout' a tenner—"

Roy walks closer to it and looks underneath and then at the side. "Sounds great, guys."

The other mechanic chimes in. "Can't shorten' with an over lockn' manifold suspension."

They go toe to toe. "I can durn well shortn,' if I reduce the thrust on nitial' takeoff."

The other elf looks at Roy and starts mumbling. "Six hunerd' foot takeoff, fourteen pallet capacity" as the other elf mechanic starts in as well. "Four fifty four, double wing, high performance—"

"Good luck with it, men." Roy walks outside as one elf crawls on top of the sled and points into the engine.

Roy spots the snowman and calls out to him. "Hey."

No answer but a small puff of smoke floats from the snowman's pipe. "What is wrong with me?" Roy asks.

The snowman finally looks in Roy's direction. "You run when it becomes difficult and the pressure mounts."

He's definitely got Roy's attention. "I have men who depend on me. My family has to understand there is a lot at risk and sacrifices will be made."

You're pretty self-absorbed...and you don't pay enough attention to the ones who love you." Roy stomps around in the snow and makes his way around the snow-man, who swings around the opposite direction. "I guess you caught the tail end of my—self-absorbed?"

The snowman takes a long puff off of the pipe and faces Roy. "Who are you really doing this for?"

"I'm trying to finish a job in there." Roy kicks snow up like a frustrated child "What gave you the impression I'm a quitter."

"You are holding your keys. Plan on driving somewhere?"

Roy shoves his keys in his pocket. "I don't have to confess to you."

Roy walks away from the snowman, but a snowball

explodes on the back of Roy's head. He looks back at the sneering snowman. "Ya asked for my advice, didn't ya?"

Jimbo catches up to Roy.

"Were you just talking to the snowman?"

"No, because snowmen *don't know what they're talking about and shouldn't meddle in other people's business*!"

The snowman shrugs.

Changes Will Be Made

A chainsaw buzzes outside Santa's room as he lays on his sofa with an ice pack on his head. He springs up and looks at his clock that falls off of the nightstand and almost hits a mouse napping below, also on a small sofa. "What now?" Santa grabs his robe and storms out.

Roz stands in front of the assembly line as it sits in pieces. Santa runs to the assembly line and looks over the parts that lay to the side. Roz puts the chainsaw back in her jacket. "I think if it was a little shorter it would cut down on time."

Santa holds up a portion that was sawed off. "You've changed all the equipment?"

Roz looks over her work. "This is the last improvement. Promise."

Santa tosses the piece aside. "Who's gonna maintain the equipment when you leave?"

She takes a huge grease gun out of her jacket. "Sutter's pretty good, I'll mention it to him if he comes back." She aims the gun. "Might want to stand aside while I—" She squirts the rollers, and it hits Corky in the face on the opposite side. Corky rolls around on the ground in pain. Roz grabs her neck and lets out a scream. Rowdy stands across the room with a pea shooter. "No more playtime."

A couple of elves stand at a wood table and carve wood figures. Jimbo tries to carve a piece but breaks it.

The elves look at each other with disgust. They hand him a small broom. "My people fought oppression and—"

The elves work and ignore Jimbo, who starts to cup their heads in his palm. "My people!" The elves slap on earmuffs, and Jimbo grabs the broom and starts sweeping. "I was on my day off."

Dissention in the Air

The guys have their faces buried in their plates and only look up occasionally to signal for more food. Jimbo tosses a bone to a moving fur ball, who gobbles it up. Crane sits a few feet away from the guys. "Maybe they can find you some elf deodorant." Roy offers up the suggestion, trying to be helpful, but Crane doesn't look up from his food.

"Don't care. Met some new friends." Crane tells him. Roy begins to say something but goes back to eating when something catches his eye from above. He looks up to see a wobbly screw and Birtnink notices. Birtnink yells out. "Look out!" A large wood column plummets to the table, knocking over bowls of food and splashing the guys. Food drips off of Roy's nose. "That could have killed me." Rowdy runs inside and Roy calls out to him. "You're lucky that your boy Birtnink was here to warn us." Rowdy and Roy lock eyes. "What happened?" Rowdy asks.

Roy stands. "Someone could've been seriously hurt."

"I'll have an engineer look at it," Rowdy tells them as he glares at Birtnink, who smiles. "Might want to look after your guests, Rowdy. You don't want them to get hurt … or even killed."

Roz raises her hand. "I'm ready for my gift now."

Frankie and Johnnie wait for everyone to fall asleep in the room and then decide to climb out the window.

Crane leans over and whispers. "Where are you guys going?"

Frankie squeezes out the window and looks back as Johnnie attempts to climb out. "Don't worry about us, O' Stinky One."

Crane whispers again and looks back to make sure nobody has noticed the escape. "You're gonna get us all thrown out of here."

"Good." Frankie tells him as he assists Johnnie out the window.

Johnnie looks back. "Throw us in jail. This ain't worth it."

"You know, you could have used the door." Crane tells them as he pulls the blanket over his eyes and they look back.

Sutter's Moment

Sutter, sullen and feeling sorry for himself, stands in front of a small cottage. He admires a young elf family through the window, who are gathered around a fire as the elf father kicks up his heels and plays the trumpet to them. Sutter trudges through the snow when a bright light shines down on him. He tries to look up, but it is blinding. He drops to his knees and begins to cry. A hand is extended.

A blind elder elf helps Sutter to his feet and walks him inside in a small but warm home made of rock. Up above, an elf pilot taps on the elf officer, who turns off the spotlight. "Just one of the ogres from the South." The elf pilot points forward. "Let's get out of here."

"Roger that." They fly off.

Inside, the blind elder elf leads Sutter to a wooden rocking chair. Sutter looks at the tiny chair and decides to sit on the cutting table. The elder elf fumbles around for a cigar, knocking items off of the counter and sending Sutter diving to catch them. He finds the cigar, lights it, and takes a long puff off of it. He offers Sutter the cigar and reaches around the counter, pretty much sweeping his small hands across it, for a bottle of wine.

"Ahh." He is quite impressed with himself as he pours the wine down the side of the glass and down Sutter's pants. Sutter taps him on the shoulder. "How about you let me do the pouring?"

Elsewhere in the North Pole, elf carolers sing in front of a gingerbread house to a terrified and trembling elf family. Jimbo stands in the back and sings in baritone, "You'll go down in *his-tor-y*." Jimbo smiles and looks down at the elf family, who all nervously tip him. One ever hands over his wallet. "Oh, thank you. Next house!" He pulls a wad of miniature bills out of his pocket. "Does this stuff spend?"

In a seedy part of the North Pole, a drunk elf stumbles down the street and bumps into Johnnie. The drunk elf spins off and quickly staggers away in fear. Outside the Sassy Santa, the North Pole's roughest bar, the elf doorman takes a long drag off of his cigarette and then points at Frankie and Johnnie with the cigarette between his fingers. "I don't want any trouble from you guys."

Frankie shrugs his shoulders and confused, looks at Johnnie.

"Why would we give you trouble?" he asks as a couple of large polar bears step outside and squares up with them.

The elf doorman waves off his bouncers. "I've seen you work. You're good. Real good. No denyin' that. Just keep your nose clean." He waves them inside. "Go ahead."

A female elf with long, fake eyelashes and stockings that go to the top of her thigh, bumps the guys out of the way. "I've watched you, too." She winks and walks inside. Music blares until the guys walk inside. The music stops and all eyes are on them. Johnnie throws out his outstretched arms. "We come in peace!" A little mumbling from the crowd but other than that, nobody is moving and all eyes are on Frankie and Johnnie. Frankie steps forward. "We are helping Santa with the..." The music resumes and elves go about their business again. They spot the elf hussy and strut toward her. An elf gambler throws his cards down and a reindeer playing cards across him throws down his cards and pulls out a wad of bills. They pass another table as a troll knocks a penguin out of his chair. The troll spots the guys and helps the penguin back in his chair.

The guys continue to walk. They spot the elf hussy and two other elf women who seductively signal them over. Johnnie grabs Frankie and shakes him. "This oughta be fun."

Johnnie walks to them and Frankie is close behind him. "Finally feel like a big shot."

They are cut off by Birtnink, who holds his arm out to stop them. "Let me buy you guys a drink!" They are confused by his generosity.

"I think I owe you that much for dragging you into this situation." Birtnink invites them over to the bar, and Johnnie slaps Frankie on the back. They stand at the bar that comes to their waists. "This is our night, Frankie."

Otto sits on a bar stool next to them, and without looking over or trying to attract any attention, he mutters under his breath. "Be careful who you associate with."

Sutter faces the elder elf as the fire reflects off of him. "Since high school, everybody has listened to this guy like he's the boss." The elder elf takes a deep breath and does his best to sound interested. "You said that he is the boss."

"Not away from work. Are we at work? Always has to be in charge," Sutter tells him as he twists on the cigar sending flakes raining down on the ground.

"I can understand your haste about the woman and losing "most congenial," but—"

"—Oh, that's not all." Sutter tells the elder elf who drops his head in his hands and then fumbles his way to the sink to clean dishes. "There's more?" Sutter follows him to the sink and the elder elf grabs the bottle of wine and drinks it straight out of the bottle.

Roy Discovers What He's Missing

Roy paces in the wish room and circles the orb. He stops and looks into it, then concentrates intensely with his hands over it. Meanwhile, Wallace sits back in his motel bed and tips back a bottle of cheap booze. His tattered jacket is hung up on a hook. He stares out the window at the moon. "I want that factory, Santa." Roy watches him through the orb and places his hands over it, careful not to go too far. Wallace slowly looks up and sees Roy's face peering down. "*Argh!*" Wallace crawls to the corner of the room and begins to cry. Roy stands over the orb making faces. "You've been bad, Wallace. *Bad!*" Roy laughs to himself and takes a step away. He stops as though he forgot something. He looks into it again as Sam appears. Sam kneels by the bed praying. "I just want my daddy back home."

Roy looks down, then leans close to the orb without touching it again but backs away, not wanting to be seen. Sam clasps his hands and squeezes his eyes shut. "I also want to be taller." Roy laughs to himself as he can see Judy tuck Sam in bed. Sam turns over and closes his eyes as Judy looks up. "Please come home, Roy."

Roy taps lightly on the orb and sparkles hover over Judy, who wipes a tear from her eye. "I'm sorry, Roy."

Roy takes a step back as multiple visions of children appear in the orb.

Johnnie rides on Frankie's back as they clear the dance floor, laughing and singing. Frankie downs the rest of his drink, and dribble goes off the side of his mouth. Johnnie takes a cigarette out of a polar bear's mouth, takes a long drag, and then hands it back. The elf hussies strut off inside the musty, dimly lit club that smells of cheap cologne.

"Where are ya going?" Johnnie leans back against the mahogany bar. "C'mon, we're big shots." He signals over the bartender. "Set me up, Spike."

Jimbo hands the small bills out to his group of carolers. The smallest one gives him a hug. "Gonna miss ya, Jimmy."

"That's Jimbo, but I guess it doesn't really matter." Jimbo waves goodbye and walks back through the snow to the toy factory as they all wave back.

Negotiations

Santa sits at the large oak table mulling over Birtnink's latest proposal. "How much are they asking for?"

Birtnink sits on the opposite end and looks over multiple documents that are spread out and completely covering the end. Elder elves study their documents as Otto sleeps with his head back. Otto abruptly awakens out of deep slumber, wipes the slobber from his mouth, and grabs a handful of papers. "Concur...Yes. Troll immigration needs to be addressed." Birtnink holds a pen in his hands and slides it down in front of Santa. "It's not how much you're paying them, it's how much you'll get in return."

Santa picks up the pen and focuses on the signature line. He takes a deep breath and begins to press the pen to the paper when Rowdy bursts in the room. "Roy has left us."

Santa stands, and Birtnink slams the desk. "But the contract!" Birtnink runs down to Santa's end of the table. "I told them to leave," Santa tells Rowdy, who is visibly upset. "If it weren't for them, we wouldn't even be close!"

Birtnink goes toe to toe with Rowdy. "Close doesn't deliver Christmas."

Rowdy does his best to control his anger as Birtnink backs off and waves the contract. "I need them, Santa."

Santa walks off. "I need to get some rest. I'll make a final decision tomorrow."

Birtnink murmurs under his breath as he glares toward Rowdy. "You'll end up just like your father."

Time to Leave or Deliver

Corky stands at the jail cell bars with an elf police officer. "So you were at the Sassy Santa last night?"

Frankie lays on a collection of cots used for all the elf inmates. He tries to open his eyes. "What am I doing here, Brubaker?" Frankie tosses his tiny blankets aside. They land on a couple of shivering elf inmates sleeping on the cold concrete floor. Corky grips the bars, leans in close, and glares at Frankie, who scratches himself and takes in his surroundings. "You know what you have done?"

Frankie rubs his temples. "I hope this doesn't violate my probation."

Johnnie, naked but covered around the waist with a wreath, awakes in the empty workshop as he is sprawled out over a worktable. Wayne, emotionless and face painted blue, stands in the corner of the room looking out over the floor. His eyes dart back and forth as if keeping watch and then still again.

Johnnie holds a clump of hair in his hand. Birtnink walks out and stands over Johnnie. "Shouldn't have had so many eggnogs."

Johnnie struggles to open one eye. "How'd you know it was eggnog?"

Birtnink scrambles off. "I'll arrange a sled for you guys today!"

Santa limps out with his hair draped down his shoulders. "Your men were supposed to have left last night. Please get your crew and have your bags packed by noon. I'll send for transportation."

Johnnie, looking at the hair in his hand, breathes a sigh of relief until Santa turns around. His head is shaved in the back except for the word, "Tigers" that is dyed in orange with black trim.

Santa turns back around and glares at Johnnie. "Oh, and when you see Rowdy, tell him he's fired, as well."

Johnnie stretches, the bones popping with every move. "Where's Roy?"

Sutter stands in front of the entrance of the cave that has two large gargoyles perched high on the mountain with bones for teeth overlooking him and the valley below. He walks inside. Trolls look up from their fire and snarl at him, though slowly backing off. "Seems I found what I was looking for." Sutter stands in front of them, almost daring one to throw him out. "We gotta talk."

Rowdy Steps It Up

Roy stands at the terminal window waiting for a sled when Rowdy walks up. "Have room for one more?" Roy paces, looking for the next sled, and doesn't respond. Rowdy looks out the window, watching the snow blanket the tarmac and mountains in the distance.

"You've been here all night."

"I tried and failed." Roy goes back to gazing out the window.

"You could have taken a sled hours ago."

An elf vacuums around them.

"I had to think on it," Roy tells him.

"Your men depend on ya." Rowdy says as he pulls the plug on the vacuum and sits down.

"Not in the mood and not staying." Roy looks at his watch and gazes outside as the sleds that come and go.

"Don't blame ya if you run. Seems like you've made a habit of it." Rowdy tries to pick a fight, but Roy doesn't budge. If anything, he seems to drift off into the white blanket that covers the mountains.

"My family misses me."

Roy turns to Rowdy. "Why did I come here, Rowdy?" Roy backs into and then sits down on a small bench.

"Same reason anybody else would have. You thought that your gift would be a miracle…a second chance, or better yet, hope."

Roy likes this and smiles to himself. "Sounds like what I've been chasing all my life."

"Can't blame ya for trying." Rowdy says as Roy takes the seat next to him.

"I know that Birtnink wants you out," Roy tells Rowdy, but Rowdy quickly fires back. "We could have done the job. I thought you Americans worked longer hours. More disciplined."

Roy waves it off. "Aaahh, not at all. Na. You've got the wrong group."

Rowdy springs up and thumps Roy in the chest. "Help me make that miracle happen, Roy."

Rowdy thumps him again, but even harder. "Birtnink wants me out like he wants you guys out. Our destiny is in our hands! We can't let him win, Roy!"

Roy thinks about it but slumps. "We would never make it."

Rowdy is now jumping up and down on the chair. "How about that American ingenuity I've always heard about?" Rowdy shakes his fists. "Win one for the Gipper!"

Roy can't resist his enthusiasm. "We always seem to find a way to win, don't we?"

"Darn right! C'mon, Roy."

Roy looks down as Rowdy hops down and looks up into Roy's face. Roy looks him squarely in the eyes. "Let's make Christmas happen!"

Roy picks up his bag and walks out with Rowdy, who runs back and plugs the vacuum back in. He winks at the elf cleaning lady. "Carry on."

Birtnink's News

Elves sit around smoking, drinking coffee, and playing cards when the phone rings. An elf picks it up then holds it against his chest. "Hey, guys, Birtnink is on the way with good news!" The room erupts in cheers. An elf tries on a uniform as the gingerbread men fight over the remote control.

Birtnink walks through the door of the elf room holding a contract. "Santa is more desperate than ever with only one day left. He'll sign tonight." Birtnink walks the length of the bed. "You will all get five percent more."

An elf jumps up. "You said ten percent!"

"I tried but could only get five," Birtnink says, but not very convincingly.

"What do you get out of this?" an elf asks.

"I did all the work," Birtnink exclaims, but there is a murmur amongst the elves. Birtnink is hit with a sock. Another flies his way. He takes a step back as a couple of more socks hit him in the face. A barrage of socks hit Birtnink as he struggles to find the door. "You duped us!" an elf calls out.

Roy walks up to Crane in the mine shaft and grabs his pick from him. "No more."

An elf miner stops what he's doing. Crane looks back at the others. "No more. " Crane waves at the miners. "Stop what you are doing!" Crane rings a large bell and waves at them to follow. They drop their tools and walk out of the cold and dark shaft.

Rowdy, Roy, and Crane walk to the shop and pass Frankie, who is being lectured by the snowman. "There is no excuse for your actions!"

"Hey, someone drugged my drink." Frankie tells him.

"That's exactly what I'm talking about!" The snowman slaps Frankie across the face, snow splashes against his cheek.

"Meet us in the shop." Rowdy tells him.

"Be there in a minute." Frankie returns his attention to the snowman. "So, some people don't mature past the third grade?"

The Contract

Santa sits at the large oak table as little green men climb back on the globe and rest from exhaustion. Santa twirls his pen as he looks over the contract.

"So how much are they asking for?"

Birtnink slinks closer to Santa. "It's not how much you're paying them, it's how much you'll get in return."

Santa reaches across the table. "Give it here." Santa looks back up at Birtnink. "You realize that I will have to bypass a third of my children in order to meet your demands?"

Santa touches South America on his globe, and it becomes blackened out. The small green men look at each other until Santa spins the globe and they all go flying. "Sign of the times ... everyone is feeling it." Birtnink assures him.

Hammering can be heard outside, and a mouse tries to drag the pen away but Santa grabs it. He looks over the contract.

"Sign it!" Birtnink's expression is demonic.

More hammering and Santa goes to the door. "Sign it for me." Birtnink pleads.

Santa runs out, finding Rowdy, Roy and Crane working on the line. "You've been replaced," Birtnink tells them as he turns off the equipment. Roy drops his hammer. "We came here to do a job."

"The elves are going back to work," Birtnink says.

"The job is not complete," Roy tells Santa.

Roy goes to the machines and looks over them. Rowdy walks over and turns them on. "Let's make some toys."

Santa looks over them as a couple of elves have walked out and are putting on their uniforms. "I told you to leave," Santa tells Roy.

Defiant, Roy wipes the sweat from his brow. "We will when we're finished."

Santa walks out the back to the snowy white garden with small frozen pools, shrubbery dotted with icicles, and trees that stand fifty feet tall. He desires an escape from the pressure that mounts.

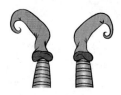

Wallace Still Doesn't Get It

Wallace is sitting on a bus, crouched between the seats. He tries to sit up but quickly grabs his neck. "Arrrgghhh!" A small child looks down on him from the seat behind his. A man looks back and observes Wallace, whose hair fires out in every direction. "You look like hell, boy." Wallace tries to ignore him and sits up while the child still stands over him. He looks down to find a few beers in a bag and then quickly clutches his head as if it were gonna explode. The man continues, "And your hair looks like a crow's nest." The child slaps his lollipop against Wallace's suit jacket.

"Why?...I just ask why?" The child tosses the lollipop, and it hits a large man sitting a few rows ahead of him in the back of the head. The large man walks to the back as the boy cries and points at Wallace.

"Oh, no. It wasn't me—" Wallace sees a fist coming his way and *pow*! Darkness.

Roz Gets a Makeover

Mrs. Claus slowly takes off Roz's jacket and sets it the side. "You know, you're not one of the guys." Mrs. Claus dabs a little blush on Roz.

Roz, looking in a mirror for the first time in years because she was afraid of what would look back, is lost in her reflection. She likes the color on her face. "Sorry it didn't work out."

"I knew it would come sooner or later," Mrs. Claus tells her.

"I think we are all a little burned out," Roz says as she loosens up, and Mrs. Claus takes out a brush. The brush squeals and then is buried into Roz's hair. "You look so pretty with a little red on your cheeks."

Wallace walks next to the road with his thumb out. He stops and looks to the sky when *splash*! A car drives on as water, mud, and ice drip from his face. Wallace's arms hang at his side as though they are too difficult to lift. He continues walking down the road.

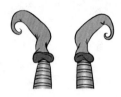

No Time to Waste

Roy and Rowdy hammer away. They finish a toy and set it aside. Roy looks over the completed toy and then at Rowdy. "It's a start." Wayne, Johnnie, Jimbo, and Roz walk out with their luggage. Roz puts hers down and looks over the toy. "What are you doing?"

"Making toys. Wanna join?" Roy asks her.

Roz laughs to herself and has an idea they might be staying, judging by the tone in his voice. "Been ordered out of here." The alarm sounds and instant chaos erupts. Roy tosses his tool down and walks out.

Roy stands on the opposite side of the fence from Sutter who is surrounded by a hundred, fearful trolls. "I was worried about you." Roy tells him.

Sutter nods at the trolls that reluctantly stand behind him with crude tools. "You need some extra help?" The trolls step forward, mucus and other bodily fluids flowing from their oversized mouths. Elves observe from some of the stores and decide to follow and help.

"Can always use some extra help…pending they clean up a little." Roy grabs the fence post and Sutter joins him. Rowdy is next to grab hold, and the trolls help out.

The fence post rips out of the ground, throwing earth in every direction.

Local elves with tools follow the trolls with Sutter,

Roy, and Rowdy leading the way as they make their way back to the shop.

Wayne finishes painting a toy soldier and grabs the hand of an elf. "Blue."

Sutter bursts through the door. "We have a job to do, and I brought some fellas who never seem to get invited to the party." Trolls walk through the door and look over the shop.

Sutter stops and looks at his clothes and then turns to Rowdy. "We have to do one more thing." Sutter nods at the trolls. "Just tell them what you need."

The trolls hold up their tools.

"You got it, boss!" Rowdy yells out.

Sutter yells at the guys to follow him. "Come on, guys."

Jimbo drops his bag and walks with Sutter as Birtnink tries to stop them. "We made a deal!"

"Wait 'til Santa gets back. I'll enjoy it when he personally throws you and those bums out." Birtnink waves the contract as though he had accomplished his goal at the guys and skips out.

Frankie walks in with the elf officer, who takes off his jacket. "What was he so excited about?"

"Glad you could make it." Roz says.

"Heard there was some work to do." Frankie goes to his workstation. Roz pulls a hammer out of her jacket and then takes the jacket off and tosses it aside. "Word travels fast."

"All of us!" Sutter barks at Frankie as they walk out of the toyshop. He reluctantly follows.

Santa tromps through the snow. Mrs. Claus steps in front of him. "Mr. Claus." He stops and looks into her large eyes and stern look. Almost as a whisper, she tells him, "Don't let this all get to you."

"Don't let it get to me? Don't let it get to me?"

Mrs. Claus grabs him and holds him tightly as Santa wraps his large arms around her. "We've had worse."

Santa grumbles, and Mrs. Claus continues, "Like when the elves went on strike. Or when we had that winter."

Santa lets go. "I've already sent them away."

Mrs. Claus takes his hand. "I think there used to a man who shows his compassion." She leads him back to the toy factory. The fence is torn away.

Santa looks at the fence and then the shop. "What is going on?" The elf security guard throws his hands up, and Santa runs to the workshop.

The guys walk back in with their elves uniforms on. Wayne grabs a paintbrush and a toy soldier. "Let's get to work, boys." Wayne's eye twitches as he dabs the paintbrush.

Roy calls out to the trolls and elves, "We have a Christmas to deliver!"

Johnnie goes to the line and winks at Corky. "Step aside."

Corky makes room for him. "Let's do it."

Jimbo jumps in next to Rowdy. "Friends?"

Rowdy tries to squeeze his shoulder, and Jimbo tries to help him by squatting a little lower. "Little higher up." Sutter sneaks in behind Rowdy and takes over. Rowdy tries to conceal his laughter and takes a step back. Sutter cracks his knuckles and looks as though he's wanted to do this for a long time. He grimaces and then grabs the muscle and Jimbo screams out, "What have they been feeding you?"

Santa frantically runs up to Roy. "What is going on?"

Roy continues to work. "Get on the line!"

"What!" Santa can't believe he heard this, and Rowdy is there to back Roy up.

"You heard him." Rowdy signals for an elf to move aside.

"*I'll be right back!*" Santa walks to his room and the room full of workers look at each other. He disappears into the room, and Roy continues to work. Santa quickly reappears with his tools in an old wooden box. Santa rolls up his sleeves. "You needed tools?"

Roy looks at the small hammer. "Sorta getting used to it, but if you've got tools, send 'em over."

Roy clicks his fingers and some seventies funk music plays, much to the others' delight. The speakers wear afros and sway to the music. Frankie smiles to himself and grabs another toy. Roy and Santa stand side by side hammering wheels on wagons.

"Might need a little help in the states. Got a factory I can use?" Santa jokes with Roy. "Not sure if you'd want this one." Roy wipes sweat off his forehead.

"I can get my hands on equipment." Santa tells him, but Roy is wrestling with the next wagon and trying to get a wheel on. "Let's enjoy Christmas for now."

Outside of the shop, a troll snatches up a pony and starts to take a bite out of it until Sutter waves at him. He slowly puts it down, and Sutter winks at him.

Sleds are loaded up next to each other with gifts. An elf walks by each one with a checklist. A penguin slides by the elf, handing him a list, but keeps on sliding.

Inside the warehouse, the abominable snowman takes a tiny toy off the top shelf and hands it to a troll, who hands it to an elf, who hands it to a mouse. The mouse scurries off with it towards the toy shop.

Frankie turns to Johnnie. "We aren't gonna make it … gotta move faster!"

Roy looks at his watch. "C'mon, guys!"

Birtnink picks up a toy doll that is halfway done. "These toys are not being built correctly!"

"Beat it, Birt," Santa tells him. Santa looks up at the clock and continues to work. He stops and takes a break when the elf door slowly opens. Roy notices and looks back at Santa. "We might have company."

The elves file out one by one, and Birtnink tries to stop them. "What are you doing?" They shove him aside as they walk toward their workstations. Sutter slaps Roy on the shoulder. "We're at full steam, guys!"

They slap high fives with the guys. Sutter takes a cookie, winks at the server, and tosses the cookie behind him. A troll catches it and eats it.

The troll grabs the rest of the cookies and the tray. "Yumm, yumm... *burp*."

Santa turns to Rowdy. "Make sure those sleds are ready to go out at O five hundred!"

Rowdy runs out.

An elf hands out cookies, but Roy and Crane refuse them as they continue to work.

Sutter and Wayne carry boxes across the room.

Crane breaks Santa's hammer. He slips it back into the carpenter's box.

Santa works with intensity on a toy soldier arm. It snaps on. "Ho, ho, ho!"

Corky nudges Santa. "Uh, Santa?" Santa holds the doll up. It is a toy soldier with one teddy bear leg and a cowboy leg with chaps. Santa shrugs it off and grabs another. "It's been a while." Roz stands at the assembly line and hands a hammer to an elf, who puts on his apron. Santa has a checklist in his hands. "We aren't gonna make it unless—"

Sutter cuts him off. "We've only got a few left but someone has to stay behind."

Toys rolls off the line and Johnnie helps put them in gift boxes as Frankie slaps a ribbon on them.

A Job Well Done

Corky sits atop Jimbo's shoulders and holds the star for the Christmas tree. He places it at the top, and everyone claps.

Johnnie, in a panic, feels his pointed ears then waves at Santa. "Uh, Mr. Claus."

Santa looks up. "Yes, Johnnie." Santa looks closer. "Oh, yes." Santa rings a small bell, and two elves run out. They both wear metal gloves. "Wait a minute." Johnnie is panic-stricken and begins to fight them off, but they lead him away.

Roy and Santa toast each other with hot chocolate. "You are a true leader."

"I couldn't do it without those guys," Roy tells Santa. "And especially Rowdy."

Roy offers Rowdy a handshake, and he responds with a hearty grip.

"You guys need to get going." Rowdy tells them.

"You're gonna be okay," Santa assures Roy.

"I'm gonna stay behind," Roy tells him.

"You have a family to get back to."

Crane steps forward. "I don't." Roy is confused and Crane continues. "Was gonna tell ya, Roy... the missus walked out on me, and the step-son hasn't talked to me in a couple of months."

Corky holds a long list and marks through the name "Zzzmerr. Almost there!"

"We'll figure something out," Santa tells Roy until a blood-curdling scream echoes through the halls.

Frankie runs into the room where Johnnie sits at a table and the elves stand beside him. Johnnie looks up. "Their gloves are cold."

Frankie laughs at him and slaps him on the back. "You scared me…brother."

"Thanks, Frankie," An elf hands Johnnie a mirror and he admires their work. "It's normal. Look, Frankie. No more scars." Johnnie thinks to himself, *I liked the scars.* Actually, a couple of the small ones on his chin and cheek were from when they fought as children. Johnnie hops off and goes to join the rest.

Crane leans over to Roz. "You looked really nice today, Roz." Roz wipes a little black soot off of his chin but it trails past his cheek. She looks it over but doesn't bother. "Thank you, Roger." Crane looks down at his shirt and then tucks it in.

"You never called me Roger before."

"And you looked nice in that little elf uniform." She smiles at him as he sheepishly looks away.

Santa holds up a mug of cider for a toast. "To the men who made it possible!" Crane fires straight up and holds a toast. "To a team effort, fellas!"

The elves hold their cups as high as they can hold them. The guys join in. Santa walks behind Rowdy. "I would also like to introduce my new lead man. Your father would be proud."

The guys clap as Santa places the ribbon over Rowdy's shoulder. Roy makes his way around and hugs Rowdy. "Ya made us all proud."

Birtnink stomps his feet and breaks a candy cane. "What? This was only temporary! And he almost ruined Christmas!"

Roy looks at his watch. "You guys have a sled to catch!"

"What are you gonna do?" Jimbo asks Roy.

"I'm staying with Rowdy. Someone has to watch over the equipment for at least another couple of days," Roy tells them.

The men and Roz rush out as all of the elves wave, and Otto sips his whiskey. "Let's get loaded up!"

Elves taxi sleds onto the runways as others take off. The guys rush out on the tarmac. Otto approaches them. "Hey, uh, if you see a short guy, can you send him back?" They throw their bags on the sled and load inside. Roy gives way to Sutter, who stops at the sled entrance and waves Roy on. "I left a gift for you inside."

Roy thinks this is odd but goes inside to retrieve it. Roy looks around the back as the others settle in. He checks under the seats and in the luggage rack. "What gift?" All of a sudden, it hits Roy and he is jerked back. "Wait a minute." He tries the door, but it is locked and the sled is moving. "Open this thing up." Roy looks out the window as Sutter waves goodbye and screams out at him. "I want to make people happy. Pretty much what I have been lacking!"

Roy locks eyes with Sutter's and Sutter smiles back. "I'll be fine." Roy waves goodbye as this is the first time he has witnessed Sutter as not only happy, but content. Rowdy gives a thumb up and walks with the sled.

The mouse, one arm in a sling, waves with his free arm. The elf locals wave goodbye. All the guys and Roz gaze outside, except for Wayne, who sits silent in the corner staring at his fingertips. The elves walk toward them, clapping in unison. They are walking from everywhere, giving their ultimate approval. The clapping grows stronger as the sled pulls forward and passing

multitudes of elves. Roz gets a little teary eyed until—
"What a weird place. Let's get the heck outta here." The
sled is jerked upward and they are off.

Back Home

Back at the bowling alley, Wallace, ragged and worn, walks in and spots the bartender. Bristo sips on a soda through a straw and watches television.

Wallace is barely able to produce the words with his extreme cotton-mouth, but he manages a coarse tone. "Where's Hopkins?"

The bartender finishes a glass and grabs another. He smiles at Bristo but turns to Wallace. "Ya mind moving? My friend is watching the television."

Wallace slowly looks over and the site of Bristo hits him like a ton of bricks.

Hundreds of sleds travel through the night loaded with gifts with bright bows. Inside the sled, Roz admires herself as she looks in a compact mirror. The elf pilot comes over the intercom. "Prepare for landing and, uh, we hoped you enjoyed your visit to the North Pole."

Roz looks back. "Gonna miss those guys."

Roy walks down the middle of the aisle. "Gonna be okay, Wayne?"

Wayne, beady-eyed and buzzing like a bee, smiles at Roy. Roy thinks about if for a moment and then slaps Wayne hard across the face. Wayne holds his cheek and loses his glossy glaze. He thinks about it for a moment. "Uh, thanks, Roy."

Roy takes the handcuffs out and Frankie and Johnnie put their hands out, but he tosses them over the side.

"You guys can work with me if you want. I don't have much, but I'll pay ya what I can." Johnnie isn't sure if this is a trick or for real, judging by his expression.

"You're not gonna tell the parole board, are ya?"

"What would I tell him, Johnnie?" They look at each other then exchange a handshake. "You're an okay guy, Roy." Johnnie tells him. Roy laughs to himself. "Keep that between us, 'cause I got a reputation, ya know." Johnnie looks at Frankie.

"No, I didn't know that." Frankie answers, and Roy laughs at them. He gazes out the window at the lights of Detroit below, wondering what his family is doing at the moments before Christmas arrives at their house.

Crane takes a piece of coal out of his pocket. He rolls it in his palm, then tosses the coal out. Jimbo slaps Crane on the shoulder, and Crane shakes his hand. Roy slides in next to Crane. "Why didn't ya tell me?"

"About the missus?" Crane stares at the ground and Roy nudges him to continue.

"She, uh, left me, and my boy doesn't talk to me. Tired of the lifestyle. I've never had anything to offer them." Roy pulls him close, and then looks out at the stars that fly overhead. "You've always had a lot to offer everyone."

"Thanks, Roy.

Wallace carries Bristo out of the bowling center. He looks up, and the handcuffs narrowly miss him. "Ha! My luck is changing!"

The coal crashes on Wallace's head. Wallace staggers

a few feet but holds on to Bristo. "I didn't travel four hundred miles round trip to let you go."

The sled slides down the street throwing snow and slush out the side as people stop and stare. It comes to a halt, and Dirty Santa peers inside from the sidewalk. The door opens and he jumps back, dropping his bottle. Roy is the first one out and takes a deep breath of the air filled with smog and exhaust. "Home sweet home."

One Naughty, Others Nice

The men walk out and go their separate ways as Wallace limps toward them. Baby Ralph, hysterical, rushes toward them flailing his arms.

"Weird stuff around here lately, Roy." Baby Ralph walks with Roy when Johnnie approaches him. "Have a nice Christmas, Roy, Crane."

Crane shakes his hand. "You too, Johnnie."

Wallace bursts in the middle of them but they keep walking. "Glad that you could make it back."

"Hey, Wallace…Bristo. Weird stuff, huh, Baby Ralph? Has anyone been around or …?"

Baby Ralph grabs Roy by the collar. "Little men runnin' around." Roy turns and notices Wallace clutching Bristo to his chest. Baby Ralph, speechless, points at Bristo and runs back to his mom's house at a full sprint.

"Don't make any sudden moves or the elf gets it," Wallace tells them. Roy realizes that Wallace is a desperate man and even though he would never do anything to Bristo, he needs to be negotiated with.

Roy stops. "You can have the property. Just let me have him."

Bristo sips on his drink and actually seems uninterested in the situation. Wallace looks at the sky and then around the area but does not loosen his grip on Bristo. "Little men? You're all insane."

Roy reaches out to Bristo. "Just let me have him." Roy

takes the key off the keychain and begins to hand them over. "Now let me have him." Crane offers his assistance and tries to keep Wallace calm. "How 'bout we take a fishing vacation?"

"Open up a tackle shop." Roy tells Crane while Wallace keeps a safe distance. "I'm not here for no stupid fishing vacation. Just give me what I came for." Wallace says as he notices someone is missing. "What happened to Sutter?"

"He no longer works for you," Roy tells him when *whack*! Wallace goes down, and the bartender shoves a club in his back pocket and takes Bristo. "Sorry. Just, uh…lookin' out for my friend." Wallace tries to pick himself up but staggers and falls again. Wallace holds his head and whines. "I would've given him back."

The Payoff

The others go on about their business and Roy unlocks the door. "I just wanted to take a few things and you can have her, Wall—" Roy opens the door and is about to give Wallace the key when a ray of golden light catches his eye. "Uh, guys." Roy stares inside as Crane rushes to see from behind him. Roy pulls the key away as Wallace stumbles forward reaching for it.

Roy walks in, but a red strand knocks him and Crane down. "What the—?"

The red strand is a huge ribbon tied in a bow between two poles and blocks the door. Roy unties it and walks inside.

Roz is speechless as she stands in front of the bridge. Cars zoom past overhead. A small house sits under it. She speaks softly to herself. "A large doll house?"

She pulls out one of many keys and walks to the front door. She opens the door, and it has all the makings of a small cottage with a kitchen, bathroom, and open room with bed and nightstand. She steps inside and feels the warmth and comfort of her own home, knowing she belongs there. On the nightstand is a book, *How To Succeed In Business*. She looks up. "Thanks." Tears that have been waiting for a long time roll down her cheek.

The equipment is brand new in the warehouse and sparkles as Wallace looks at it and then at Roy." What have you done?" He grabs Roy by the collar. "You didn't tell me about this!"

"You should have asked when you made your Christmas list," Roy tells him.

Crane, as if in a trance, walks to the corner of the building. He stands in front of a huge white blanket draped over something large and wrapped in another huge red ribbon. A four-by-four foot Christmas card is propped in front of it with his name on it. Crane's mouth is wide open, but he manages to say, "Oh, boy." He staggers toward his gift but is bumped aside by Johnnie who has just sprinted over from the halfway house. "What did you guys get from Santa?"

"Santa?" Wallace asks as nobody pays attention. Roy turns a large switch, and the machinery fires up and sparkles as the lights go on.

Frankie drives a green Harley inside. "You won't believe it!"

"What is going on here?" Wallace asks.

The bartender runs inside with Bristo on his shoulders and evidently received a nice gift or gifts, as well. "Merry Christmas!" He spins around with Bristo holding on tightly. "Yahoo!"

Crane pulls the blanket off and it floats off of the mobile home. A fishing reel and tackle box sit beside it amongst other boxed gifts with ribbons on them.

Crane turns to Roy who drops his head. "Do you see this?" Crane grabs the fishing pole and casts. Roy is happy for Crane. "He knew you needed to get away in comfort."

Wayne runs inside and slaps Roy on the shoulder. "They did it! They did it! And I've realized the meaning of Christmas from a spiritual point of view." Wayne holds up a skeleton key, and Roy looks closer. "A key to the proverbial kingdom?"

Wayne laughs at Roy's response. "No, a key to the back door of the comedy club on fifth and Marburry. It's my life's ambition to perform there on Thursday nights … I'll expect you on the front row." Wayne runs over to Crane's toys.

A sullen Roy walks around admiring his coworkers. "Happy for ya, Wayne."

Jimbo bursts inside. "You guys gotta see what I got!'

Crane places his hand on Roy's shoulder. "You gonna be okay?"

Wallace drags himself around the floor. "I didn't get anything."

Roy starts for the door. "I have to get going, Crane."

"This should be the happiest day of your life … ya know, the factory. She's brand new."

Roy looks up and strains to see the exit door as two figures stand in it, one short and one medium height. Roy walks slowly toward the door but his pace builds until he is running. Wallace lunges at him as he is certain Roy was in the sled. "It was you."

The guys run around the factory. Wallace can't seem to find which direction to go. "Did I get anything?"

Judy and Sam stand in the doorway. Roy hoists them up for a brief moment and then puts them gently down. "I've missed you two so much."

Crane turns and goes to Roy as Roy tosses him a set of keys. "I'm gonna be taking some time off. I need a couple of good managers."

Crane slaps him on the shoulder. "I'm always by your side, buddy."

Roy looks over the factory. "*Merry Christmas!*"

Wallace begins to cry and then sits in the middle of

the warehouse. "Where's my gift?" He looks at his torn and tattered jacket and takes it off. He tosses it over his shoulder, stands and limps out.

The guys run outside bumping Wallace to the side, and Roy looks up at the roof. Santa leans over and gives a wink. A small ballpark for kids is being built with a huge ribbon on it next door.

Rowdy sits in the corner of the room of the toyshop and smiles to himself. Corky passes him. "Want to get out and get a bite to eat?" Corky offers.

Rowdy looks up and smiles at Corky. "Sure you want to be seen with an outsider? I mean I was only brought in to do work with the scabs."

"Ya ever get tired of this music?" Corky asks.

The Christmas music stops. Corky looks back at Rowdy. "C'mon, let's get out of here."

"Nah, I've gotta get back." Rowdy takes in the moment, and Corky walks to the door.

"If you change your mind…"

Rowdy pulls out a hammer and observes it, and then pulls a toy leg out of his pocket and tosses it on the table. He jumps up and grabs his bag in the corner of the room. He walks to the door, taking one last look back when—

"Heading somewhere?"

Rowdy turns. "Dad?"

Rowdy's dad walks in with the mouse and a portrait.

"Someone told me you might need this."

Rowdy grabs his dad and hugs him. "We did it, Dad."

"Proud of ya son. Let's go celebrate with the rest of the folks."

Rowdy walks out and sees all the townspeople out celebrating in the town square with Sutter in the middle of them. Christmas was delivered once again.

The Off Season

Elves stand around another elf, who holds a device that looks like two small hubcaps attached to each other. He speaks into it and distorts his voice and sends it higher and then drops it lower with all the elves laughing at him. "Hi, I'm a big, dumb, goofy American . . ." He stops when Sutter walks in the room. "No offense."

"Hey, guys." Sutter waves and picks up the voice object and then speaks into it. "Hello." He pulls it away and hands it back to the elf. "Let me know if you guys are up for some ice fishing or cards tonight." Sutter stands over them getting blank stares. "Well, okay. I'll see you guys later."

Sutter walks out and the trembling elf hands it to another.

Birtnink shovels reindeer poop in a suit that is caked in mud. He looks back with a scowl. "*What are you lookin' at?*" Birtnink scoops up poop and heaves it into a pile as he is hit with a snowball. Elf children who taunt him run off and he runs after them until he is cut off by a troll who reaches down for him.

"No!" The troll, wearing a security uniform with badge, backs off, and Sutter runs over and hands a shovel to Birtnink. "Rowdy said you need that done by four . . . hop to it."

Birtnink, grumbling to himself, walks back to the

stables, and Sutter slaps the troll on the back. Let's go get some beer. First one's on me."

Birtnink tosses a bridle over the fence and then goes over himself, landing on his butt and rolling to his side in pain.

Sutter and the troll walk past a granite column where the fence once used to sit. The sun begins to set and the star resides in its usual place, throwing light over the bustling city that waits until another Christmas and the adventures it brings it.

Birtnink limps down the hall with his bridle, when he sees an image of Wallace in the orb from out of the corner of his eye. He walks to it and stands over it. Wallace looks up and whispers, "If you are up there, Santa, I know all about these guys who helped ya." Wallace looks around as if not to be noticed. "They're criminals not to be trusted." Birtnink leans over the orb and Wallace backs away but steps back up to it. "I'll do anything for you if you help me."

Birtnink smiles to himself and walks away, when Corky approaches him with a piece of Jimbo's luggage.

"We need you to take this to the sled at hangar two."

Birtnink gladly takes it. "Would not be a problem."

"I see a change in attitude," Corky admires about him.

"Anyway I can help." Birtnink saunters off toward hangar sniveling to himself with an obvious plan in mind.